"We have called you here to help us," the Triple Being announced. "The universe has been invaded by a strange, amoral creature called the Lord of the Flames. He has been trying to find out as much about this universe as possible, and he thinks nothing of completely perverting or destroying a culture to get this information.

"The Lord of the Flames is particularly interested in the planet Earth. Earth's long-standing Empire of Toromon has grown weak; it may have crumbled beyond hope already. And the Lord of the Flames hovers nearby . . .

"The reason for his interest is clear. He is making ready to begin a war in our universe, beginning with Toromon. We can only have three direct agents on Earth: this leaves a fourth open for infiltration. And among those four agents, there will be a traitor—the Lord of the Flames himself!"

CITY OF A THOUSAND SUNS

by
Samuel R. Delany

ace books
A Division of Charter Communications Inc.
A GROSSET & DUNLAP COMPANY
1120 Avenue of the Americas
New York, New York 10036

CITY OF A THOUSAND SUNS

An ACE Book

*For John and Marjorie Brunner,
for, at least,
the loan of the typewriter*

Author's Note

Revising one's old fiction because of one's new ideas suggests a confusion of art and journalism—at any rate, a mistaken notion of the way art gains either effect or worth. Revising old fiction to clarify ideas now past creative ferment is a tricky business at best. Writers better than I have tried both and botched them.

Written between the end of 1961 and the beginning of 1964, each of the *Towers'* three books went into production practically as it was finished; by the time I was nearing the end of book two, book one was in type. But I had already made notes on changes I would have liked in volume one, particularly in the prologue, several of the vignettes in chapter one, and the expository material of chapter six. And, in chapter eight, I had invented a rather clumsy language for one of my subcultures which, by now, I realized, admitted no development. Because, however, no changes could be made, some preposterous robots were hauled on stage at the end of book two to explain (by exploding) some of the looser ends from book one. And a few incomprehensible grunts were strewn through book three in deference to that obstreperous tongue.

In 1966, for the British edition, I incorporated my notes, removed the robots, and from the rest excised some clumsy sentences of exposition, now superfluous, and the language.

That, essentially, is the version here.

I do whittle when I re-read, lopping an adjective here, pruning a prepositional phrase there, adjusting a bit of syntax elsewhere. Poets from Keats to Auden, in this way, have practically wrecked some of their best poems. But the *Towers* is prose. And I would hazard that, save the changes mentioned, chapter by chapter, paragraph by paragraph, sentence by sentence through ninety-eight per-cent of the work, the substance is one with the original edition.

And I suspect, with all its flaws and excesses, it is time to stop whittling.

—SAMUEL R. DELANY   *San Francisco, 1970*

CITY OF A
THOUSAND SUNS

CHAPTER ONE

WHAT is a city?

There is at least one on the planet Earth, isolate among deadly seas, alone on an island near a radiation-pitted continent. Some of the sea and the land at the edge of the continent have been reclaimed: among these silent tides and still plains there is an empire. It is called Toromon. Its capital city is Toron.

Halfway around the universe, in a dispersed galaxy, is another . . . city.

A double sun throws twinned shadows from a tooth of rock jutting in the sand. The gullies sometimes shift in the rare breeze. The sky is blue, the sand lime white. Low on the horizon are streaks of clouds. And down the steep side of one powdery dune is the . . . city.

What is the city?

It is a place in the sand where a field of energy keeps the octagonal silicate crystals in perfect order, lined axis end to axis end. It is a place where a magnetic compass would spin like a top. It is a place where simple aluminium has the attractive capacity of sensitized alneco. And although, at the moment, it housed hundreds of inhabitants, there was not a building or structure of any kind in it. The sand was no longer smooth, and only a microscope could have detected the difference in the crystalline placement.

Responding to the psychic pressures of those who observed it, at times the city seemed a lake, at others a catacombe of caves. Once it had appeared a geyser of flame, and occasionally it looked like buildings, towers, looped together with elevated roads, with double light glinting from thousands of sunward windows. Whatever it was, it stood alone on the white desert of a tiny planet halfway across the universe from Earth.

A meeting was being called in the city now; and with merely a turning of attention, the inhabitants met. The presiding intelligence was not single, but a triple entity much older than any of the others present. It had not built the city. But it dwelt there.

We have called you here to help us, it began. *Simply by being here you have already contributed greatly. There are only a few more of you to arrive, but we thought it better to begin now than to wait.* To one group at the meeting, immense, thirty-foot worms, the city seemed a web of muddy tunnels and the words came as vibrations through their hides. *As we have explained before, our universe has been invaded by a strange, amoral creature whom we have called till now the* Lord of the Flames. *So far he has only engaged in scouting activity to find out as much information about life in this universe as possible.* A metallic cyst received the words telepathically; for him the city was an airless, pitted siding of rock. *But even through his methods of experimenting, we know him to be danger-ous. He thinks nothing of completely perverting or de-stroying a culture to gain his information. We have tried to drive him out, and to keep the various cultures of the universe intact. On your several worlds, as our agents you have all had contact with him. And you have all had brief contacts with each other.* To the fifty-foot eyestalks of one listener the atmosphere of the city was tinged methane green. *He has been gathering information for a full-scale attack, but since we have dogged him to each planet, we have been able to see the information he gathers. Each of your cultures was undergoing some serious political and social upheaval when he chose to examine you. His method of observation in each culture has been to activate the elements that would push the upheaval a little too fast, would bring it to its conclusion a little too rapidly. Then, oddly, his point of concentration would be not the work- ings of economic or social upheaval itself but rather an intense study of the personal life of some socially alienated individual, a madman, an upper echelon political figure, often an outlaw, a dispersed genius at the edge of society.* To one living crystal in the city the words of the Triple Being came as a significant progression of musical chords. *Now we wish to discuss one particular incident of his observation.* A sentient cactus shifted its tentacles and beheld the city almost as it was in reality, a stretch of pastel sand; but, then, who can say what was the reality of the city. *You have all arrived here except our agents from Earth, and we want to take this opportunity to discuss their specific situation.* To a casual observer of the meet- ing, the statement that the Earth representatives had not arrived would have seemed a flagrant oversight; one of the attendants was an attractive, auburn-haired woman with wide hazel eyes. But a minute examination would have shown her slim almond-nailed fingers, her cream and honey skin to be a bizarre cosmic coincidence. Internal examination and genetic analysis would prove her a bisexual species of moss. *Self-contained and self- providing, the empire of Toromon has rested on Earth for five hundred revolutions about the star Sol. The upheaval that Toromon went through was a complex economic, political, and psychological reorganization coupled with a tidal wave of technological advances in farming*

3

methods and in food production that the degenerate, thousand-year-tired aristocracy was unable to redistribute. "Tidal wave" was the metaphor that a web-footed, triple-lidded marine creature from a world all water heard; to others it was "earthquake," "sandstorm," "volcano." *Their solution was to stimulate a situation which existed only in the libraries from the time when the whole planet was populated with nations like theirs: they simulated a war, a war that would rid them of their excess, in energy, in production, in lives. The vestigal skeleton of a military organization that had survived from before their isolate period (when just such real wars had completely demolished other nations, leaving Toromon alone) was enlarged to a tremendous force, armies were recruited, equipment was prepared, and a vast fantastical war was staged near the radiation-saturated rim of their empire, controlled by an immense random computer situated in the ruined remains of a second city in their empire called Telphar. Because of the radiation around them, evolution has run wild in Toromon, and there is one atavistic section of the population that has regressed to a point that race had passed three million years ago, while another segment has jumped a million years ahead and has become a race of giants with many telepaths among them. The telepaths tried to remain above this war, but were at last dragged into it. Our agents, a telepath among them, convinced them—in an effort to find some other solution less destructive than this mock war—to establish a momentary telepathic link among all the inhabitants of the empire. The fact that the war was not real has come out among the people. The results have been too violent to predict accurately. The whole structure of Toromon was weak; it may have crumbled beyond hope already. Outlaw bands of malcontents—or malis—roam the country.*

There was an attempt to establish a new, young king, and for a while that worked, but the governmental system had been designed to rule a peaceful, calm nation, not a nation at war. A strange life-form composed solely of thermal vibrations oscillated pensively in the city, listening, contemplating. *The reason we go into this situation in so much detail is because of the strange action of the* Lord of the Flames *when he encountered Toromon. First of all, his attempts to bring the situation to a rapid termination were immensely more violent and destructive than in any of his previous endeavours with other worlds. We, who can sense the energy of his concentration, realized that the intensity of his observation has quadrupled. Whatever he had been looking for desultorily among your worlds, he found in Earth. Our agents drove him out once and he returned. They drove him out a second time; he still hovers near, ready to invade again. We can only have three direct agents on a planet: we can only house ourselves in three minds. But with the help of the telepaths, we contacted two more—Tel and Alter—who became our indirect agents for a while. One of our indirect agents, Tel, was killed in the mock war, and so there are only four people left on Earth who are our contacts. As I said, we can only inhabit three of their minds at once; this leaves one, already used to contact extra-terrestrials, open for infiltration; this time we are sure that the* Lord of the Flames, *on his third return to earth, will choose one of our own agents, whichever one is left outside our protection. If we let them know directly the results would be disastrous to their own psyches. Therefore, our contact, already rare, will have to cease entirely after our next message.* A great bird ruffled its golden feathers, blinked a red eye, cocked his head, and listened. *The reason for the* Lord of the Flames' *interest in Toromon is clear. He is making ready to begin a war in our universe; he is now trying to find out all he can about how a life form of this universe conducts itself in a war. And this war of Toromon is a pure war, because there is no real enemy. Well, perhaps we can learn something too. We have the advantage of knowing where to look, for everyone in this city is so much more akin to each other and to the Earth men than is the* Lord of the Flames *that ideas such as "intelligence," "compassion," "murder," "endurance" mean nothing to him; he must learn them by alien observation. Similarly, he has characteristics of which we have no idea. To further our own understanding, we have requested our agents to bring with them three documents, products by three of the most sensitive minds on Earth; the* Poems *of Vol Nonik, the* Unification of Random Fields, *by Dr. Clea Koshar, and* Looms of the Sea, *a Final Revision of the History of Toromon, by Dr. Rolth Catham.*

There was silence in the city, and then a faint life-form spoke, a form that existed only as a light-sensitive virus who saw from the star-wide waves of novas to the micro-micron scattering of nutrinos, a life form disturbed occasionally by a fragment of ionized hydrogen, a loose photon, the aethric hum of a spinning galaxy eternities away from its home in cold, inter-galactic space: "What will stop them from getting these . . . works?"

Then the Triple Being returned: *These works, remember, are by the most sensitive minds of Earth and will never reach the common man as books or periodicals, and among our four agents, there will constantly be a traitor, the* Lord of the Flames *himself.*

And a universe away . . .

6

. . . and she was beautiful, beautiful with sun through the cracked window caught in her falling hair, beautiful with her closed eyes, her olive lids, darker than the rest of her face, the rest of her skin, which was beautiful with colours like honey and the blush of kharba fruits going from white to pink, before they become speckled, orange, ripe; beautiful with textures like velvet, like polished, brown stone where her knee was drawn up and the skin tight; and where her body curved slightly towards him, at her side, and the skin was loose—like velvet.

The cracked pane in the window made a jagged line of shadow over the floorboards, up the side of the bed, across the crumpled sheets, a serpent of shadow on her stomach. Her lips were opened and her bright teeth were faintly blued by the shadow of her upper lip.

She was beautiful with shadows, the long violet ones that fell over the waterfront streets where he had walked with her last night, beautiful with light, the glare of a mercury light which they had stopped under briefly to talk to a friend of his——

"So you went and got married after all, Vol. Well, I thought you would. Congratulations."

"Thanks." They both said it, and his voice, low tenor, and hers, rich alto, were even musical together. "Renna, this is my friend Kino. Kino, this is my wife, Renna." He spoke that solo; like a single instrument after a chord, it implied symphonies to come between them.

"I guess you won't be having so much to do with your old gang any more." Kino dug a dirty finger in a dirtier ear. "But then, you never were a gang man really. Now you can sit around and write poems as you always wanted to, and enjoy life." And when the grimy youth, too old for urchin, too young for derelict, said "life" he glanced at her, and all the yearning of his restless age flamed in his eyes and lit her beauty.

"No, I'm not a gang man, Kino," Vol said. "And you remember Jeof, don't you? What with that stupid feud between him and me, I decided that this is as good a time as any to drop out of the whole mali business. We're going to be moving to the mainland in a couple of days. There's a place there we've heard about that we'd like to look at."

Kino moved a bare toe around a cobblestone. "I wasn't gonna mention Jeof, but since you did first, I guess I can say I think getting out is a good idea. Because he is a gang man, to the root of every rotten tooth in his jaw." Suddenly he ducked his head and grinned apologetically. "Look, I gotta go some place. You just don't let Jeof see her." He made a motion towards Renna, and with the motion Vol looked at her, her dark skin pale under the light of the mercury lamp; Kino was gone, and she was . . .

. . . beautiful with shadow again as they walked through the dark streets of the Devil's Pot and at last turned into the ram-shackle tavern-boarding-house, beautiful as they stepped into the hall and darkness closed over her, blackening details. Just then someone opened the door at the end of the hall and a wash of yellow threw her into silhouette as she walked a step ahead of him, and he learned with his eyes as he already knew with his hands that the shape and outline of her whole body—waist, breasts, neck, and chin—were beautiful. They had gone together to his room.

On the wall was an exquisite picture she had done of him, red chalk on brown paper. On the rickety table in front of the window was a sheaf of paper. The top sheet bore the final draft of a poem that was, in its exquisite way of word and bright image, a portrait of her.

He sat cross-legged in the crumpled, body-warmed bedding, now, and looked at her beside him until his eyes ached with keeping his lids up, looking not to miss the beauty of her breathing, the faint flare of her nostrils, the rise of her chest, the movement of her skin a millimetre back and forth across her collarbone as she breathed. His eye, flooded with her gloriousness, filled with tears. He had to blink and look away.

When he saw the window again he frowned. Last night there had been no crack.

He followed the line down the window, where the two pieces of the pane were fractionally dislocated against one another, to the lower left-hand corner: a sunburst of smaller cracks arrayed a three-inch hole. Some object had knocked a corner from the window. He stood up and went to the table. Broken glass glittered over the paper. (''As I would my words glitter,'' he thought.) He picked up the rock with the strip of cloth wrapped several times around it. When he unwrapped it and read the words, blurred where the ink ran into the fibre, there was no glitter. Instead, small trip hammers struck against a hard ball of fear he had carried for so long now, held it in the alternation between declarative and imperative:

''Saw Jeof after you. You get. Says he'll eat you for breakfast. Go now. He means it. Kino.''

He spent two seconds trying to figure out how they could have slept through the sound of the rock, then spiralled to the conclusion that the rock flung from the street was what had awakened him at first. The thought was cut off by a crash on the first floor. He turned, and saw her open her eyes. Beneath those olive lids, brown pools, where gold flecks surfaced in the proper light, she smiled. The smile vaulted towards him across the grimy boards, ricocheting from clapboard wall to stained clapboard wall (where the only thing beautiful was perhaps her red-chalk portrait of him) and from the elation that filled him, even his dawntired irises relaxed, and against the rods and cones deep in his eyes, the room brightened. "And I love you this morning too," she said.

As his own smile came, a dark thought made an ominous rippling in his mind; she also wakes to a sound that she did not hear, seeing only me, as a moment before I saw her.

Below, furniture toppled again.

She asked him a question with her face, silently, lips parting farther, tilting her head on the pillow. He answered her with the same frown and a shrug of his flat, naked shoulders.

A rush of feet on the stair; then the sharp voice of the woman who ran the boarding-house, protesting along the hall: "You can't just break in here like this! I run a respectable boarding-house. I have my licence! You ruffians get out of here. I tell you I have my . . ."

The voice stopped, the wave broke, something hit the door, hard, and it flew open, banging the foot of the bed. "Good morning."

"What the hell do you want?" he said.

There was no answer, and in the silence he looked at the squat neanderthal, disproportionate torso, bowed legs; the cheek had been laid open six times, and the scars crossed and crossed again. There was a wide maroon scab over the left eye from a recent injury. The edges of the scab were wet. Ugly, he thought. Ugly.

The weight shifted from right foot to left, slowly, and

the hip that was up went down, and the one that was down went up. "I want to make you *miserable*," Jeof said, and stepped into the room. Three others stepped in behind him. "I see you got Kino's message." He laughed. "We took it away from him last night when he made his first try." Then a repentant look superimposed itself over the grin. "But then I thought maybe I'd toss it up here this morning before I came to say hello." Jeof took another step into the room, looked sideways, and saw where she sat in the bed, eyes wide and golden, skin pale, hands, mouth, eyes and shoulders terrified. "Well, *helloooo!*"

Vol leapt forward—

—his stomach wrapped itself around a jutting fist. He grunted, closed his eyes, and hit the floor. When he opened them, a second later, there were at least another six people in the room. Two jerked him upright again. Then Jeof hit him in the stomach once more, and as his head flopped forward the hand came back the other way, knuckles first, and slapped his face up. "Now," Jeof said, turning away from Vol again. "As I was saying, hello."

His years on the streets of the Devil's Pot had made Vol an accurate street fighter. It had also taught him that if the situation is hopeless you save your strength in case the miracle that'll get you out of it happens, and you can use that strength to recover. And it was hopeless.

So at first when Jeof walked towards her, and she cried out, he only stood. But then the cry turned into a long, steady scream. Suddenly Vol was screaming too, and fighting, and their voices had lost all music and become dissonant and agonized. He fought, and nearly killed one of the men who held him, but there were three others around him who broke four of his ribs, dislocated his shoulder, and smashed in one side of his jaw.

"No," said Jeof, making a calming gesture with his hand—there was blood on his hand, and she couldn't scream now because the cartilages of her larynx were crushed, "Don't kill him. I just want him to watch what we do to her." He looked around. "One of you guys come over here and help me now." They used their hands, then their whole bodies, and then the double gleam of a power-blade came from a hidden scabbard, the bottom of the hilt was flicked, and white sparks glittered up the double prongs.

A minute after that, mercifully, Vol lost consciousness. They couldn't even beat him awake. So they left.

Half an hour later Rara, the woman who ran the boarding house, got up enough courage to look into the room. When she saw the naked man crumpled in front of the table she said, "Good Lord," and stepped inside. Then, when she saw what was left on the bed, she couldn't say anything, and just stepped backwards with her hand over her mouth.

The man's hand moved on the grimy floorboards. "Oh, my good Lord," she whispered. *"He's* alive." She ran towards him, beating out of her mind a picture of the two of them together as she had seen them even yesterday (drinking from the same tin cup at the downstairs sink, walking with loosely coupled fingers, laughing at each other's eyes). She kneeled over him, and his hand moved to her foot.

Got to get him out of here before he wakes up, she thought, and tried to lift him.

Vol was at the point now in drifting unconsciousness where the pain of his cracked ribs jabbing at his lung was enough to wake him. He opened his eyes, and looked blankly at the face of the woman bending over him. It was a strong face, though the other side of fifty. A brown-red birthmark sprawled over her left cheek. "Rara?" he spoke her name with just a hint of inflection, and the bruised jaw, swelling now, kept all expression out of his face.

"Mr. Nonik," she said. "Come with me, won't you?"

He looked away, and when his eyes reached the bed he stopped.

"Don't, Mr. Nonik," Rara said. "Come with me."

He let her raise him to his feet and walked with her to the hall, despite his agonized arm, despite the fire on the right side of his chest.

Rara saw the limp and recognized the impossible angle at which his arm hung. "Well," she began, "we're going to have to get you to General Medical pretty quick. . . ."

Then he cried out. It was a long cry, wrenched up from inside him; it changed in the middle, rising nearly an octave to a scream (like a trapped boar in a quicksand pool whose cry goes from the hope of struggle, rising through sudden understanding, into final terror and submersion). "Screee-*aaaa* . . ." Vol sank to the hall floor. He shook his head; tears ran down his face; but he was quiet.

"Mr. Nonik," Rara said. "Mr. Nonik, get up."

Again he stood. The silence started chills on her back. She supported him down the hall. "Look, I know this won't mean anything to you, Mr. Nonik, maybe. But listen. You're young, and you've . . . lost something." He heard her through a haze of pain. "But we all do in some way or another. I wouldn't say this if it hadn't been for what happened a month ago, that moment when we all suddenly . . . knew each other like that. Since then I guess a lot of people have said strange things, that they wouldn't normally. But like I said, you're young. There

13

are so many people that we lose one or another, whom we think are . . . are like everyone who saw you two knew you thought she was. But you'll live." She paused. "I had a niece, once, that I loved as much as a daughter. Her mother was dead. Both she and her daughter were acrobats. Then, four years ago, she disappeared, and I never saw her again. I lost her, lost a person I had brought up since she was nine years old. And I'm alive."

"No . . ." he said, shaking his head now. "No."

"Yes," she said. "And so are you. And you'll stay that way. At least if we get you to General Medical." Suddenly the despair that she had been trying to keep out of her voice, keep away from him, broke through. "Why must they do things like that? Why? How can they do it now, after that moment when we all knew?"

"For the same reason they did it before," he said flatly. "Just like you," he went on, and she frowned. "They're trapped in that bright moment where they learned their doom. But they won't get me. They won't."

"What are you talking about?" she asked, but his voice (or perhaps it was the sound of the words themselves, the double "o" of doom, a rare word then, that echoed the spuming sea) brought chills again.

"They'll never find me," he said. "Never!" He lurched forward—and fell a quarter of the way down the stairs.

"Mr. Nonik!"

He caught himself on the banister, and started on again. Rara hurried down behind him, but he was already at the door.

"Mr. Nonik, you've got to get to General Medical!"

He stood in the door, naked, shaking his head in animal

14

denial. ''They'll never find me!'' he whispered once more, then he was gone into the street.

Bewildered, she hesitated. When she looked she couldn't see him at all. The early morning pavement was deserted. The sun was bright. At last she gave up looking. She found an officer to bring back to the boarding-house and report what had happened.

The twin sun shone on the white sand of the city.

''When will the agents from Earth arrive?'' someone asked.

As soon as they have found their three documents, the triple voice said . . . *and if they are still alive.*

An ozone-scented breeze shifted the powdery whiteness down the side of a dune so that the subtle shape of the desert was changed again, and the only thing stable and isolate was the city.

Near the centre of Toron an old merchant sat on his tiled balcony, gazing at the palace towers, then down to the clapboard houses in the waterfront area of the Devil's Pot. ''Clea?'' he said.

''Yes, Dad.''

''Are you sure this is what you want? You've had every possible honour Toromon could offer you as a scientist, for your work in matter-transmission, your theoretical studies. I don't think I've ever said it directly to you. But I'm very proud.''

''Thanks, Dad,'' she said. ''But it's what I want. Neither Rolth nor I intend to stop working. I have my Unified Field Theory to complete. He will be working on a new historical project.''

"Well, don't stand there. Call him out here."

She walked back into the house, then emerged a moment later, hand in hand with a tall man. They stopped before the marble table at which Koshar sat. "Rolth Catham, you wish to marry my daughter, Clea Koshar?"

"Yes." The answer was firm.

"Why?" And response was quick.

Catham turned his head slightly, and the light glinted on the transparent plastic case of his cheek. The fraction of his face that was mobile flesh smiled, and under it the direct gaze of Koshar wavered. "That's not a fair question," Koshar said, "is it. I don't know. Since that . . . second when we all . . . well, you know. Then, I guess a lot of people have been saying things, asking things, and even answering things that they wouldn't ordinarily."

The embarrassment, Clea thought. Why must they all speak of that blind moment of contact that had blanketed the empire that second at the end of the war with embarrassment. She had hoped that her father would be different. It wasn't embarrassment at what had been seen, but at the newness of the experience.

" 'Why?' is never an unfair question," Catham said. "It's partly because of what we saw at that moment."

Catham spoke of it without fear. That was one of the reasons she loved him now.

"Because we'd known each other's work. And because during that moment we knew each other's mind. And because we are the two people we are, that knowledge will serve us for heart and soul as well."

"All right," Koshar said. "Get married. But . . ."

Clea and Rolth looked at each other, smile and half-smile leaping between them.

"But why do you want to go away?"

Faces grave once more, they looked back at the old man.

"Clea," Koshar said. "Clea, you've been away from me so long. I had you when you were a little girl. But then you were away at University Island so much, and after that you turned right around and wanted to live alone, and I let you. Now the two of you want to go away again, and this time you don't even want to tell me where you're going." He paused. "Of course you can do it. You're twenty-eight years old, a woman. How could I stop you? But, Clea . . . I don't know how to say this. I've lost . . . a son already. And I don't want to lose my daughter now."

"Dad—" she began.

"I know what you're going to say, Clea. But even if your younger brother Jon were alive—and everything would make it seem that he was dead—even if he were, if he walked in here right this minute: for me he would be dead. After what he did to me, he would be dead."

"Dad, I wish you didn't feel that way. Jon did something stupid, clumsy, and childish. He was a clumsy child when he did it, and he paid for it."

"But my own son, in the penal mines, a common criminal . . . murderer!" His voice fell to grating depth. "My friends do me kindness by not mentioning him to me today. Because if any of them should, I couldn't hold my head up, Clea."

"Dad," Clea said, with entreaty in her voice, "he was eighteen, spoiled. He resented me, you . . . and if he is alive anywhere, eight years will have made a very different man from the boy. After eight years you can't keep this up against your own son. And if you can't hold your head up now, perhaps that's your problem, and has nothing to

17

do with Jon." She felt Rolth's hand on her shoulder, a gentle warning that her tone, if not her words, were passing into that dangerous field of outrage, like particles moving into a random energy field, darting and unpredictable. She drew back from the feeling.

"I won't forgive him," her father was saying. He clasped his hands together. "I can't forgive him." He averted his eyes from her, staring into his lap. "I couldn't. I'd be too ashamed——"

"Dad!" she had turned from the outrage now, and the word came with all the love she felt for him. She saw his body, back, neck, arms, fingers, locked in self-protective inward curves. "Dad!" she said again, and held her hand out to him.

The curves broke, his hands separated, his eyes lifted. He did not take her hand, but he said, "Clea, you say you've got to go away, and you say you don't want anyone to know where you are. I love you, and I want you to have anything you want. But at least . . . letters, or something. So I'll know you're all right, so I'll know . . ."

"It can't be letters," she said. Then she added quickly, "But you'll know."

Catham said, "We've got to go now, Clea."

"Goodbye, Dad. And I love you."

"I love you," he said, but they were already entering the wide doors of the house.

"I wish I could tell him," Clea said when they reached the front door, "tell him that Jon was alive, tell him why we have to go so secretly."

"He'll know soon enough," Catham said. "They'll all know."

She sighed. "Yes, they will, won't they. That great, monstrous computer in Telphar will let them know. They could all know now if they wanted, but they're too embarrassed. Rolth, for three thousand years everyone has tried to find a word to differentiate man from other animals; some of the ancients called him the laughing animal, some the moral animal. Well, I wonder if he isn't the embarrassed animal, Rolth.''

Her husband-to-be laughed, but with half humour. Then he said: "I've asked you this a hundred times, Clea, but it's so hard to believe: you're sure of those reports?''

She nodded. "The only ones who've seen them are a handful of people who were intimately involved in the computer construction. I was only allowed in by the skin of my teeth, more because of that final mix-up at the palace then anything else. But it makes me ill, Rolth, ill that I had anything to do with that monster.'' She let out a breath as they passed from the shadow of the balcony on to the colonnaded street. "But then I've worked through that guilt business already, haven't I.'' It was a question that needed only the momentary reassurance of his hand tightening around hers. "Rolth, they've tried four times to start disassembling it. But it won't work. Somehow it's protecting itself. They can hardly get near it.''

She turned, waved to her father on the balcony, and then continued down the street.

"How, I won't question,'' Rolth said. "It's got all the unused equipment, armaments, and so forth for a full-scale war in its control. But, 'Why?' Clea. You're the mathematician. You know computers.''

"But you're the historian,'' she answered, "and wars are your department.'' She glanced once more at the tiny figure on the balcony that still waved after them. "I wonder how long it will take him . . . them to learn.''

"I don't know,'' he said. "I don't know.''

Above, the transit-ribbon scribed a thin black line across the sky.

When old Koshar, on the green balcony, saw them disappear he sighed. Then he did something he hadn't done for a long time. He went in, called the taxi service, changed into inconspicuous clothes, then shuttled along the radial streets of the city to the waterfront. He stood around quietly while the launch pulled out with the afternoon shift of workers for the Koshar Aquariums.

Once he paused at a corner while a transport rumbled by with "Koshar Hydroponics" in large green letters over its aluminium side. He stopped outside a building, the cleanest and tallest in the area; it was the offices of Koshar Synthetics.

Later, walking the thin, dirty alleys of the Devil's Pot, he stopped in front of one of the combination tavern-boarding-houses. He was thirsty, the afternoon was hot, so he entered. A number of people apparently had had the same idea, and the conversation was going at the bar. A friendly voice beside him said: "Hello, old man. Haven't seen you here before."

The woman at the table who had spoken to him, close to fifty, had a large birthmark on one side of her face.

"I haven't been here before," Koshar said.

"I guess that would explain it," Rara answered. "Have a seat." But he was already moving towards the bar. He bought a drink, then turned with it, wondering where to go, and saw the woman sitting by the door. So he went back and sat down at her table. "You know, a long time ago I used to spend a lot of time in this area. I don't remember this place though."

"Well, I've only had it here about a month," Rara explained. "Just got my licence. I'm trying to drum up some steady business. Being friendly is real important in business, you know. Hope I see you around here often.''

"Um," Koshar said, and sipped green liquid from his mug.

"I tried to start a place some years back. Took it over from a friend of mine who passed away. But that was just when the malis were getting started, and they busted the place all up in a raid one night. Now, here I am just started a couple of weeks and I've had trouble already. Some of them broke in here this morning, one of those gang-feud things. Of course officers are never around when you need them. Killed a girl." She shook her head.

An argument had started at the bar. Rara turned, frowned, and said, "Now what do you suppose that's all about?"

A wiry man whose face was cracked from wind and sand spoke loudly, while a woman stood beside him, her green eyes fixed on his face. But he was looking at another man. "No," he was saying. He made a sharp, disgusted gesture with his hand. "No, it's rotten here. Rotten."

"Who are you to say it's rotten?" somebody laughed.

"I'll tell you who I am. I'm Cithon the fisherman. And this is my wife Grella, a fine weaver. And we say your whole island is rotten!"

The woman put her strong hands on his shoulder, her eyes imploring for silence.

"And let me tell you something else. I used to live on the mainland coast. And I had a son, too; he would have been as good a fisherman as I am. But your rottenness lured him here to your island. You starved him out on the mainland, you seduced him here with the aquarium-grown fish. Well, we followed him. And where is he now? Is he sweating himself to death out in your aquariums? Or is he running with one of your mali gangs? Or maybe·he's draining the good sea salt from his body in your hydroponic gardens. What have you done with him?'' What have you done with my son?''

''Damned immigrants,'' muttered Rara. ''Hold on just a second, will you?'' She got up and went over to the bar. The man's wife was trying to pull him away, and Rara assisted her. The man got really nasty before they got him out.

Rara came back, brushing her hands on her skirt. ''Immigrants,'' she said again, and sat down. ''Now I'm not saying anything against them; some of them are good people, some of them are not so good. But some of them are nuts like that. Funny, that woman looked awfully familiar. Like something I might have swept off my doorstep once.'' She laughed. ''But then, all those green-eyed mainlanders look alike. Oh, are you leaving? Well, come back soon. This is a real friendly place here. Real friendly.''

Outside, Koshar stopped once in front of a wooden fence, scabbed with the remains of peeled posters. Across the remnants of blurred shibboleths someone had scrawled in red chalk:

> YOU ARE TRAPPED IN THAT BRIGHT
> MOMENT WHERE YOU LEARNED YOUR DOOM

The wild irregular shape of the letters (or perhaps it was in the words themselves, the palatals of ''that bright moment'' clicking against the soft labials, like the clock of coins in a random matrix) made him feel strange.

Old Koshar turned up the street, his heart half-broken.

A universe away, white sand blew down the dunes.

What is the city?

It is a place where the time passes as something other than time. It is a place where the mechanical movements of spring, cog, and gear would slow to a veritible stop. The same is true with a clock of blood, bone, muscle, and nerve. Yet the psychic flashing of photon against photon travels at normal if not accelerated speed.

"But why is this isolated empire of Earth so important?"

"Are they so technologically advanced that this paper on Random Fields will give us a weapon to vanquish the *Lord of the Flames?*"

"Will this historical work predict for us the outcome of our own great war?"

"Is there no other art among all our cultures that teaches so much compassion, that fixes life's place in the universe so brilliantly as these poems?"

A score of minds, in their ways and words, formed a barrage of bewilderment. For answer came a triad of laughter. *The Earthmen are important because the* Lord of the Flames *is among them now,* and the "now" is an inexact translation for the reverberating concept of cross-sectioned, inter-gallactic time with past and future patterning implied. *Yet if these Earthmen arrive their very arrival will herald our victory over the* Lord of the Flames, *and there will be no need to study their documents, other than for your own edification. If they do not arrive, then we are defeated.*

Bewilderment among them grew to concern.

You will see why, the triad voice said. The double sun dropped towards the horizon, and there was silence in the city.

CHAPTER TWO

"PUT your head back."

He put back his head.

"Now bring your knees up and roll backwards."

He rolled, feeling the torque of his shifting weight from his wrists to his taut shoulders. Slowly his feet came down, his toes brushing the mat.

"Fine," she said.

He let go of the rings. "Think that's enough for today?" he asked her, grinning.

"More than enough," she said. "You don't want to work at it too hard, Jon. That's no good either. Let yourself ease into it. You're doing superbly already. Where'd you get that co-ordination?"

He stepped off the mat, shrugging. "The muscle I got first when I was in jail, digging tetron ore at the penal mines. The rest—I don't know."

"You really amaze me," Alter said. "The way you've been sticking to this tumbling business is impressive. And the progress is more so."

"It's something I wanted to learn," he said. "I don't like being clumsy. Let's shower and then get something to eat."

"Fine." She smiled.

They left the gymnasium and walked along the tiled hall to the showers as a bunch of youngsters came from an adjoining hall in bathing suits. One girl, thick bodied and

24

low browed, snapped a towel at an extraordinarily tall youth with a flat, equine face. The others laughed, and then continued down the hall.

"Have you seen that girl swim?" Jon asked. "You wouldn't think it to look at her, but her speed is fantastic."

"I saw her through the observation porch this morning," Alter said. "You're right. That hundred yards was pretty amazing."

Just then they passed two boys loitering by the wall. One had small features pocked with acne. They were also looking after the swimmers. "Damned foreigners," one muttered, his face hardening.

"Catch them walking around the Devil's Pot at night," the other one said and sneered. Then he made a grinding gesture with his fist against the tile.

Jon and Alter exchanged frowns and separated at the shower rooms.

Ten minutes later, his skin steamed and his hair damp, Jon stepped out on to the concourse. Shifting jets of water from the aluminium fountain clashed in the sun. Alter was already standing there. Her bare tanned shoulders, her long legs and sandled feet moved slightly in the act of waiting. A breeze cooled his face, and at the same time he saw wisps of her white hair leap to the side.

A couple stopped by the fountain, stared at the base, frowned, and moved on. When he reached her he, too, frowned. "What's that?" he asked.

"Where?" She turned to look. A scowl of surprise formed around her light eyes. "I didn't see that before!"

Someone had written across the dull metallic surface in whitewash:

> YOU ARE TRAPPED IN THAT BRIGHT
> MOMENT WHERE YOU LEARNED YOUR DOOM

25

"What's that supposed to mean?" Alter asked.

Jon read it once more. "I don't know. But it makes me feel funny."

Somewhere something buzzed.

Across the concourse one person looked up, three more; then by dozens, eyes turned to the whining sky.

Above the transit-ribbon, two, then three, then four silver flashes hurled through the clouds.

"Aren't they awfully low?" Jon said.

"Scouting planes?" Alter suggested.

A small bead of light dropped from one of the airships. When it hit, there was a silent flash among the city towers. Seconds later the sound came, and with it, restraint broke and the screams started.

"What the . . . !" began Alter.

For five seconds the sound came on, a concussive rumbling.

"That's the war ministry!" Alter cried.

"That *was* the war ministry," Jon said. "What the hell happened?"

A broken stud of burning masonry, the remains of the tower, flickered above the hem of buildings. Chaos broiled on the concourse. "Come on," Jon said. "Let's go!"

"Where are we going?" Alter asked.

"To get something to eat and to sit down and talk."

They made their way to a side street. As they reached the corner, the news speaker grill began humming:

Remain calm, citizens. Remain calm. A tragic accident has just occurred at the Military, where, through a grave oversight, planes from Telphar carrying high explosives were rerouted automatically by a failure in the mechanism of the disbandment programme. . . .

By the time they turned into the restaurant the casualty figures were being given out.

The front window of the place they chose was two twelve-foot discs of multi-coloured glass rotated slowly in opposite directions by hidden machinery. Pastel patterns slipped across the tablecloth as they slid into the booth.

"What do you think happened?" Alter asked again.

Jon shrugged. "An accidental bombing."

"That's a strange thing to happen accidentally," said Alter.

Jon nodded.

There was some disturbance at the restaurant entrance and the two looked up.

A woman with a wealth of fiery hair had just entered. The man with her was a handful of inches over seven feet. The owner of the restaurant apparently did not wish to seat the giant—an example of the behaviour that was becoming more and more common towards the giant forest people and the squat neo-neanderthals since the release of so many soldiers from the war. The owner made his excuses with explanatory gesticulations: "But we are already full . . . my other patrons might not under . . . perhaps somewhere else you would receive. . . ." The woman became annoyed. She touched her lapel, turned it over, and revealed her insignia.

The owner stopped in mid-sentence, put both hands over his mouth, and whispered through his pudgy fingers: "Oh, Your Grace, I had no idea it was . . . I'm so terribly sorry that . . . I never realized you were a member of the royal . . ."

"We'll sit over there with that couple," said the Duchess. With the forest guard, she moved across the room to where Jon and Alter sat.

The owner preceded them like a diesel-powered slug. "Her Grace, the Duchess of Petra, wonders if you would be so kind as to allow herself and her companion . . ."

But Jon and Alter were already on their feet. "Petra, Arkor," cried Jon, "how are you? What are you doing here?" And Alter echoed his greeting.

"Following you," answered the Duchess shortly. "We just missed you at the Public Gym and then caught you ducking around the corner in all the confusion."

"May I . . . eh . . . take your order?" ventured the owner.

They ordered, the owner left, and what little interest there was from the other diners melted now that the altercation was over.

"What did you want us for, Petra?" asked Jon. He looked closely and saw that the Duchess's face was tired.

"The war," she said. "The war again."

"But the war's over," said Alter.

"Is it?" asked Petra. "It may be too late already."

"What do you mean?" Jon asked.

"You saw the 'accidental' bombing a few minutes ago?"

Jon and Alter nodded.

"First, it wasn't accidental. Second, there are going to be a lot of other 'accidents' unless we can do something about it."

"But . . ." began Alter, "there's no enemy."

"The computer," the Duchess said. "The reports have just come in. I only saw them in my capacity as adviser to King Let. Apparently the computer that ran the war has gone wild! Its self-repair circuits have made use of the radio-co-ordinators to seize any equipment with automatic controls. Until now it has only defended itself against the

28

military dismantling unit. But today it launched its first attack on Toromon.''

"How?" Jon wanted to know.

"A very imprecise explanation accompanies the report. Remember that thousands upon thousands of minds were controlled semi-hypnotically by the machine, and recorded in complete detail. Even though it killed thousands of men, it still had these mental records in its memory bank. Somehow, between its structure and function, the whole pattern of death and war was lifted from the minds of its victims and internalized by the activity circuits. The result was the bombing of the military ministry. Right now it seems to be spending long inactive periods still digesting the information. But its activity is on the increase, and what the end . . ." She stopped.

"So we're still up against ourselves," said Jon, after a moment. "Only this time in a mirror image stored in memory banks and transfer coils."

"What about our galaxy-hopping friend the Triple Being?" Alter asked. She glanced about, always feeling odd whenever she mentioned the strange force known only—if it existed at all—to the four of them. "It kept promising to help if we helped it, and we certainly have."

"But we have heard nothing from them," Arkor said. "All I can think of is when peace was declared and the *Lord of the Flames* was driven from Earth, their interest in us ceased. Whatever we do now will have to be done on our own."

"But we are going to need help," said the Duchess. "Somehow I feel that if we could find——"

It touched them, but subtly, registering on another level than perception, so that the green light from the window reflected on the silverware held for a moment the faint flicker of beetles' wings, the copper grill over the air vent for an instant was the same red as polished carbuncle, and the general flickering in the eye was a faint web of silver fire: the four were touched, three of them with the presence of the Triple Being; yet one of the four . . .

"—could find your sister, Dr. Koshar, she could be a great deal of help. She worked on the computer for a while and should know something about it; she's got the sort of mind that might be able to cut through exactly this sort of problem."

"Another person we would do well to consult," came the measured voice of the giant telepath, "is Rolth Catham. A war is an historical necessity; I'm quoting him, and he has more understanding of the economics and historical influences on Toromon than any other person alive."

The others, who had consulted Catham before, nodded, and for half a minute there was silence.

"You know," said Jon, "who I would like to find, Alter?"

"Who?"

"The person who wrote that thing on the side of the fountain."

"I've been wondering myself," said Alter, "just who thought that one up." She turned to Petra. "It was almost a line of poetry that someone scrawled over the fountain in front of Gymnasium Plaza."

" 'You are trapped in that bright moment where you learned your doom,' " said the Duchess.

"Yes, that's it," said Jon. "Did you see it on the fountain when you came looking for us at the gym?"

"No." She looked puzzled. "Someone had scribbled it across the palace wall by the gate this morning. But it stuck in my mind. That's all."

"I guess a couple of people have been writing it," Alter said.

"I'd like to find the one who wrote it first," said Jon.

"Well, before that, Jon, let's see if we can't find Catham, and your sister," the Duchess said.

"Why, is there a problem?" asked Alter. The young acrobat brushed back silver hair. Large eyes, blue-grey, blinked in her tanned face. "We should be able to find them at University Island, right away, shouldn't we?"

Now Arkor spoke. "Yesterday morning Rolth Catham resigned the chairmanship of the history department of the University of Toromon, left for Toron that afternoon, leaving no indication of what his plans were."

"And my sister, Dr. Koshar?" Jon asked.

"She quit her position with the governmental science combine," the Duchess said, "also yesterday morning. After that, nobody can trace them."

"Perhaps my father knows where she is."

"Perhaps," said the Duchess. "We haven't wanted to ask him without speaking to you first."

Jon leaned back in his chair, looked at his lap, and then up. "Eight years," he said, "eight years since I've seen my father. I guess it's about time I went."

"If you'd rather not . . ." the Duchess began.

Jon raised his black eyes quickly, tilting his head. "No. I want to. I'll find out from him where she's gone—if he knows." Suddenly he sat up. "Will you excuse me, please?" He pushed his chair from the table, walked to the entrance of the restaurant, and left.

The three remaining at the table looked after him, then back at one another. After a moment the Duchess said, "Jon has changed recently, hasn't he."

Alter nodded.

"When did it start?" asked Petra.

31

"At that moment . . ." She paused, then gave a little laugh. "I was about to say 'at that bright moment where we learned . . .' " Now her face furrowed with remembering. "It was the next day that he asked me to teach him tumbling. And he's mentioned his father an awful lot recently. I think he's been waiting for a reason to go and see him." She turned to Arkor. "What did Jon learn when we all saw each other? He's always been so quiet, such a deep person up until now. He still isn't what you'd call talkative, but . . . well, he is working hard at the tumbling. I told him at first he was too old to get really good, but he's making so much progress, I wonder."

"What did he learn?" It was the Duchess who asked now.

"Perhaps," said the telepath," who he was."

"You say 'perhaps,' " said Petra.

Arkor smiled. "Perhaps," he repeated. "That's all I can say."

"Has he gone to see his father now?" asked Alter.

The giant nodded.

"I hope it goes all right," she said. "Eight years is a long time to hold grudges. Petra, Arkor, when you teach somebody something physical, just from the movements of their body, you learn how they feel, what makes them breath deeply when they're glad, or pull their shoulders in when they're afraid; and just watching him for these past couple of months. . . . Well, I hope it goes all right."

"You and Dr. Koshar were very close to each other," the Duchess said, leaning forward over the table. "Do you have any idea where she might have gone?"

Alter looked up. "That's just it," she said. "Up until that moment at the end we were always together, talking, laughing about something. Then she went away. At first I thought she'd gone into the same sort of retreat she was in when I first met her. But no, I got a few letters, she hadn't given up working; she was happy over her new field theory, and I thought she was finally getting at peace with herself. From the last letter that's what seemed to be happening. But there hasn't been another one, and this business about her stopping her job: that seems strange.''

"Almost as strange," mused the Duchess absently, "as a country at war with its mirror image caught in a steel memory bank."

CHAPTER THREE

WHAT do you think when you're about to see your father after five years of jail and three of treasonable adventuring? Jon asked himself that: the answer was a fear deep in his throat that might slow his pace walking, drag at his tongue when he would speak. As he walked up the radial street of the city, other fears returned. There was the nameless one from childhood that had to do with a woman's face that might have been his mother's, and a man's that was probably his father's, but it was vague. At eighteen there had been a week of fear, beginning with a ridiculous dare by a treacherous friend who happened to be the late king of Toromon (and he wondered now, would he have taken the dare if it had come from another boy?) and finished with clumsy panic, a stroke of Jon's power-blade, and the death of the palace guard chasing him. Then there were five years in prison (the sentence was life, not five years) in which anger and humiliation and hate for the guards, for the faulty mining equipment, for hot hours underground with rocks scraping his hands, for the sound of tall ferns brushing his dirt-stiffened uniform as he walked to and from the shacks at dawn and sunset; but the only time in prison fear had come undisguised was when the first talk of escape began, filling the night in whispers from bunk to bunk, mouthed behind a guard's back in the infrequent rest periods that punctuated his subterranean labour. It was not fear of punishment, but of the talk itself, of something uncontrollable, the small random thing unplanned for in the tight fabric of prison life, flowering in the unregimented moment, in a free exchange of eyes, in the whispers passed in the washroom. He had tackled that fear differently, by joining the plans, helping, digging with his hands till his nails were quick-torn, counting the steps a guard took from the office to the sentry-box at the edge of the prison area. When the plan was finished only three men remained: he had been the youngest crouched in the light rain by the guard-house steps, waiting for freedom.

During the dash, in darkness, with wet fronds beating his face, there was no fear. There was no time for it. It culminated and exploded in his brain like the cyrstalline spears in a disturbed super-cooled liquid after he had got lost from the other two, after he had wandered from the jungle too close to the edge of the radiation barrier, after he had seen the spires of Telphar black on the dawn, when, unexpected, unpredictably, with neither mental nor physical defence, over the distance of a universe he was struck from the stars.

Then came the adventuring. There had been danger and he had been weary, but not afraid in the same way he was now. This small white emptiness was a negative of the black spot of terror from half-remembered childhood.

34

He climbed the long-ago familiar stairs of his father's house and stopped in front of the door. As he raised his thumb to the print lock he thought, is it through this doorway freedom lies?

It had been a long time since the lock had read the lines and whorls of his thumb: dark wood fell back, and he stepped into the foyer. He wondered if his father had changed as much as he had. If his working habits were the same he would be working in the family dining-room.

Jon walked by the wall hangings of blue cloth, the familiar chronometer embedded in the floor (the crystal had been replaced since he had last seen it), past the turn in the hall that had the strange whispering-chamber effect where you could stand thirty feet away around the corner and hear someone talking, even softly, by the coat closet, past the door to the trophy room (the wood on the panelling had been split before, now it was repaired) and into the ballroom. High, dim, it spread before him to the long, swan's-wing staircase that cascaded from the inner balcony. His sandle heels *clisped* softly, steadily, and for a moment he felt that many ghosts of himself were following him to the dining-room.

The door was closed. He knocked, and a voice said, "Who is it? Come in."

Jon opened the door. And hundreds of clocks began to tick.

Startled the portly man with white hair looked up. "Who are you? I gave instructions that nobody was to be admitted without . . ."

"Father," he said, thinking. Am I telling him or asking him?

Koshar pulled back in his chair, his face darkening. "Who are you and what are you doing here?"

"Father," Jon said again, thinking, The knowledge is

hanging in front of him like a glittering light and he is pulling back, afraid. "Father, I'm Jon."

Koshar sat forward again, both hands falling to the desk like weights released. "No."

"I've come back to see you, Dad," Jon said, thinking, Even denying it, he has admitted me. As he stood in front of the desk the old man who was his father raised his head, his jaw moving slightly as if tasting over possible words and finding them bland.

He said at last, "Where have you been, Jon?"

"I . . ." Then all this perceptions turned inward, and as clearly as he had been observing his father, he was staring at the chaotic emotions that had exploded in himself: he wanted very much to cry, a little boy lost and found in the dark, or a man lost and finding himself in light. There was a chair beside him, so he sat down, and that helped keep tears from coming. ". . . I've been away a long time, a lot of places. Jail, you know about, I guess. Then I've been in the service of the Duchess of Petra for three years, having adventures, doing a lot of growing up. Now I've come back."

"Why?" Koshar's head shook, shook as though a sledge had just struck the base of his spine. "Why? Do you want to be forgiven, for disgracing me, making me unable to hold my head up before my friends, my business associates?"

Jon was quiet a moment. Then he said, "You suffered too?"

"I, suffered . . .?"

"Five years," Jon said, softer than he meant, "I saw sunlight less than an hour a day, was yelled at, beaten; I strained in the neon darkness of the tetron pits and called up muscles I didn't know I had. I rubbed my palms raw on rock. You suffered?"

"Why did you come back?"

"I came back to find my . . ." He paused. Suddenly the resentment turned over in him. "I came back to ask you to forgive me, for hurting you—if you can."

"Well I——" Then old Koshar began to cry. It began as the dry sound of a man unused to tears, but like an empty cistern before a creaking dam, the sound filled. "Jon," he said. "Jon."

He went around the desk and put his arm tightly around his father's shoulder, thinking: the dangerous we do by instinct, by relying on training; and the hardest are done quickly, walking a familiar street to a familiar door, that moment in which we must go backward to go on. "Dad," he said, "where's Clea? I came to talk to her too."

Koshar sucked in his breath. "Clea? She's gone."

"Gone where?"

"She's gone with the history professor, from the University."

"Catham?"

"They were married, yesterday. I asked them where they were going, but they wouldn't tell me. They just wouldn't tell me."

"Why?"

Koshar shook his head again. "They wouldn't tell."

Jon went to the front of the desk, sat down, and leaned over it towards his father. "They wouldn't give you a reason either?"

"That's right. That's why I got so upset, just now, about you. I think a lot, Jon. I didn't like thinking about you in the mines, and me here, living off the ore you broke your back to pull up from the ground. That embarrassed me more than anything my friends ever could have said." Koshar looked down, and then up. "Son, I'm so glad to see you." He extended his hand across the table, and with the other took out a pocket handkerchief and wiped his face.

Jon took his father's hand. "I'm glad to see you, Dad." Just as a whirling blade cuts into the spinning bar on a lathe and hones the blunt end to sharpness, so the blunt confusion of Jon's emotions suddenly honed to a point that scribed a clean line down his being.

His father shook his head again. "Toron is a very tight, moral little world," Koshar said. "I've known that since I was a boy, and more than any other piece of information, using that has helped me become rich. Yet, it's trapped me, and held me away from you."

"There's a lot of violence outside that world, Dad," Jon said. "I hope it doesn't crash in on your world and destroy it."

His father gave a little snort. "There's no more violence outside than there is in. If I learned one thing in that moment it was that."

On the desk-communicater a yellow light blinked. Koshar pressed a button and a mechanically thin voice said, "Excuse me, sir, but an emergency report came in from the mainland. Somehow a tetron tramp stalled just outside the harbour for six hours. Its control mechanism was hopelessly fouled, and it was unable even to radio for help. While it was stuck malis from a small power-craft overran the boat, dumped the ore, and in the panic two officers were killed."

"What time was this?" Koshar asked.

"About ten this morning."

"Were the malis responsible for the stalling? Was it their plan?"

"I don't think so, sir. That's the whole thing. The tramp was one of the old radio-control ships. This morning the whole area was blanketed with an incredible interference that seems to have originated in Telphar. There are rumors that the military is having some trouble with the computer, which may have something to do with it. The malis were just passing by and took advantage of the situation.''

"I see," said Koshar. "Check directly with the military, will you, and find out what's going on, and if it's going to happen again. Send the answer straight to me."

"Yes, sir." The voice clicked off.

"Damned pirates," said Koshar. "You'd think they were trying to run me personally out of business. I don't understand this violence for violence's sake, Jon. They don't steal the ore; they just dump it and do as much damage as they can."

"It's not easy to understand," Jon said. He stood up. "If Clea contacts you will you let me know? It's very important. I'm staying at——"

"You're not going to stay here?" Surprised bewilderment broke in his father's face, and struck through to him. "Please, Jon; this huge house has been so empty since you and your sister went."

"I wish I could, Dad." He shook his head. "But I'm staying in the middle ring of the city. I have a place there, that's mine. It's easier for me to get to the places I have to go from there."

An expression wilted in his father's face. Then a deeper one flowered. "I guess I couldn't expect you to return as if nothing had happened." Over the shelves the clocks whispered to one another.

Jon nodded. "I'll see you again soon, Dad. And we'll talk a lot, and I'll tell you a whole lot of things." He smiled.

"Good," his father said. "That's so good, Jon."

Outside the sun lowered over Toron's towers, filling the deep, empty streets of the city's hub with shadow. Jon walked through the street, feeling both powerful and re-laxed. Towards the middle ring of the city the spectacular buildings of the central section gave way to more ordinary structures. Here people walked back and forth, many returning from work, and an occasional transport rolled past. Jon was three blocks from his apartment when he saw something across the street that made him stop.

Barefoot, trousers frayed, black shirt torn across his back, hair wild, a boy was scribbling letters over the wall in long slashes of chalk: *You Are Trapped in That Bright Moment Where* . . .

"You!" Jon called out and started across the street.

Hair flew back on the head, the figure whirled, paused with feet apart, arms out, then ran down the street.

"Wait!" Jon called, and ran after him. Jon caught up after three-quarters of a block, spun him by the shoulder, and pushed him panting against the wall. His forearm struck the boy's chest, and with his other hand he grabbed the boy's wrists. "I'm not going to hurt you," Jon said evenly. "I just want to talk to you."

The boy gulped and said, "I didn't mean to be marking up your building, mister."

"It's not my building," Jon said, aware of how much better dressed he was than his captive. "What were you writing? Where did you see it?"

"Uhn?" The grunt was almost a question.

Jon let go. "You started to write something on the wall. Why? Where did you hear it? Who told it to you?"

The youth shook his head.

"Look," Jon said. "I'm not going to bother you. What's your name?"

Black eyes flickered left and right, then stopped again on Jon's face. "Kino," he said. "Kino Nlove."

"You're from the Devil's Pot, aren't you?"

Kino's eyes dropped and sprang from his own rags again to Jon's clothes and then to his face. "Going back that way?"

Quick, suspicious nod.

"I'll walk part of the way with you," Jon told him. They started, Kino still wary. "You were about to write: *You Are Trapped in That Bright Moment Where You Learned Your Doom.* Right?"

Kino nodded.

"I've seen it scribbled around the city. You must be pretty busy."

"I didn't write them all," Kino said.

"I guess you didn't," said Jon. "But I want to know where you got it from, because I want to know who wrote it first."

Kino was silent for a dozen steps. "Suppose I did write it first," he said. "What would that mean to you?"

Jon shrugged.

"I *was* the one who wrote it first," said Kino, as though he didn't expect to be believed. Then he added, "I didn't say it first, but I wrote it first. Then I saw a couple of places where it was chalked where I didn't write it, and I thought that was real funny."

"Why?"

Kino laughed shortly. " 'Cause I knew it was going to happen. I knew other people were gonna start writing it too, start thinking it, wondering about it. And I thought that was the funniest damned thing in Toromon. Like you're wondering about it, huh?" His voice at once grew sullen and secretive. "Didn't know nobody was gonna come slammin' after me though, like you did."

"I didn't hurt you," said Jon.

"Naw," Kino shrugged. "You didn't." Then he laughed quickly again.

"Who said it to you?" Jon asked.

"Friend of mine."

"Who was he?"

"A friend," repeated Kino. "A murderer, a thief, a poet: he ran a mali gang for a while, over in the Pot."

"How did you know him?"

Kino raised a heavy black eyebrow. "I ran with him."

"What was his name?"

"Vol Nonik."

"When did he say this to you?"

"Yesterday morning."

Jon felt curiosity sharpen. "What sort of character was this murderer, thief, poet, mali-leader of yours? And what possessed him to say that to you yesterday morning?"

"What do you want to know for?" Kino asked. "You wouldn't believe it."

"I don't know why," Jon said. "Like you said, it makes you think. But I'll believe it."

"You're a funny guy," Kino said. "You talk strange, like a mali, even."

"How do you mean?"

"You want to know funny things, believe anything. That's what Vol told me made a person a mali. He said when a guy gets out and gets his face ground into the real world he comes up angry, wants to know how it works, and he'll believe anybody who tells him how, right or wrong."

"Vol Nonik said that?"

"Yeah. Where you been that's real, pig?"

"What?"

"Where you been in all them fine clothes you got,

where hunger hacks your belly and death tells you you ain't free, pig?'' Kino laughed again. "That's mali talk, see?''

"I've been in the penal mines," Jon said. "I've puked in the pit, pig, and that tongue you swing in your head and call mali talk is just plain old pick-pocket jabber to me. Thief's lingo's gone up in the world.''

"You were in the penal mines?'' Surprise bloomed in Kino's voice. He tapped Jon on the shoulder with the back of his hand. "Big *man*!''

"Now what about Vol Nonik?''

"I guess it won't do no harm,'' Kino reflected over a gnawed hang-nail. "You know any mali business at all?''

"My time with that was a long while ago," Jon told him. "It didn't even have the name then, and that lingo you fling around was pretty rare. I just heard a couple of guys joking with it back in the mines.''

"Oh! Well, once upon a time there were three mali gangs.''

"Spill on,'' Jon said.

"The people in these gangs are a funny bunch: lots of guys who were too messed up even to get into the army; then lots of guys who were sharp enough to haggle their way out before they got to the death-tanks; everybody's crazy younger brother; your misfit cousins; and, pig,'' here Kino made a fist and shook it "we got 'em from all over Toromon. Apes and giants from the mainland, rich kids from the middle of the city, a lot from the edge, and more from in between: you people don't want to know it, but we're growing all over this dead land. Oh, yeah, and girls.'' Kino laughed. "All them nice sweet, pretty gentle little things they wouldn't let go to war. Most of the gangs have at least a handful that run with them, cut with them, kill with them. And there are at least three gangs that don't let no studs in at all. And, pig, you watch out for them witches on a dark night by the waterfront.''

''Where does Nonik float in?''

''Three gangs,'' Kino came back, ''Vol's gang, with me there too, see. Then a gang run by an ape named Jeof. You know those apes don't quite have it all in the head, and they know it; so when they get into a gang they make up for it by being *mean*. And Jeof ran one of the meanest. Third was Larta's gang. She was one of them giants from the mainland. Nobody knows why she came, or what she was doing before. She just hit the Pot one week, all scarred down the side of her face, and that was *it*. Some people swear she can read minds.'' Kino rubbed his dirty hand down his left cheek. ''Three gangs, see? And one city block in the Devil's Pot that both Larta and Jeof wanted. This was just about a week before that Moment. There was a lot of glitter on that little strip, pick-pockets, gambling, some hard hustling, both A.C. and D.C., and the other stuff a mali can worm his way into and live off. To settle a territory dispute, what they usually do is call in a third gang who fights it out with each of the other two, and the one who wins over the third gang gets all rights. Since you're battling with a disinterested contender, it keeps it from getting too bloody, or boring. If both sides whip the third they get a fourth and start all over again. Well, Nonik was called into the middle. They fought, and Larta got the area. Her witches still have it, too. But Jeof demanded a return match with Nonik. And suddenly there was that Moment where we all knew, about the war, and each other.

''A lot of funny things happened in the malis then. Vol and a couple of others broke up their gangs. Vol had been going with a girl named Renna from the middle ring of the city, and her old lady would have had a fit over his mali gang. They met at the University. She was an artist and some sort of teacher and wanted him to go on writing and stop the violent stuff. I guess he wanted to himself, because right after the gang broke up they got married. Only Jeof didn't like this. He thought Vol was chickening out of the whole business, and he wanted his return match. Then Jeof's gang got smashed by another gang, and he somehow managed to blame that on Vol too. He swore he'd get even with him, and yesterday he did.''

"What did he do?"

"Killed Renna. She never had anything to do with any of the mali business, and didn't really want Vol to. For Vol, she was everything that was good and clean and right and orderly and . . ." he paused, ". . . beautiful. You watched them together, and it was like each one was a world in which the other wanted so much to reach, and might some day, and just in trying was beautiful. Jeof crashed into Vol's world and killed her.''

"Just like that?" Jon asked, sensing the outrage that flickered then faded in Kino's tight face. "What happened then?"

"I guess Vol went crazy," Kino said. "He ran out in the street stark naked. I was coming to see him that morning 'cause I had tried to warn him Jeof was after him, and at the corner I saw him staggering down the street with no clothes on. I didn't know what Jeof had done then, but I knew Vol was hurt. I pulled him into an alley, wrapped a sack around him, and got him to my hole—I'm sunk in an old warehouse by the docks, an abandoned refrigeration building—and got some clothes on him. I pulled what had happened out in little splinters that made him howl. He was raving about something being after him, and I thought he meant Jeof. But he meant the universe, pit-worm! That's when he said what you saw me write on the wall.

"Then he laughed. 'You tell them that,' he said, 'then see what happens. You tell them all that, and watch them squirm. But they'll never catch me now.' I was trying to hold him up and I steadied myself against one of the burnt beams on the warehouse wall. 'I got to get you fixed up,' I said. 'I've got to get you to General Medical.' His arm was all shot and his face bruised. He said, 'Let them try and fix themselves up. It's too late. They're trapped. We're all trapped.' Finally, I got him outside. Once he made me stop by a fence and told me to write what he had said on the boards. I told him we had to get to General Medical. It was still pretty early and there were hardly any people out, I was going right down the big street to get there as quick as I could when, I remember, I heard a helicopter. I glanced up and saw that it was flying awfully low. Vol was nearly unconscious.

"Suddenly the 'copter began to roar down, and a moment later it sat right in the middle of the street ahead of us. Then this woman and the weirdest guy you ever saw jumped out; half his head is plastic, and you can see all the brains and things! He runs up the street and the woman is right behind him, and he cries out, 'Vol! What happened, Vol?'

"Now I really get scared. Then I think maybe this is who Vol doesn't want to find him. The man says, 'Clea, help me with him.' Then he asked me what happened to him. I can't run, because Vol's too heavy and weak. Vol half wakes up, shakes his head, and then whispers, 'Professor Catham,' tears himself away from me. The man said, 'Clea, help me get him to the 'copter.'

"Then I decided to run. Once I turned around, and they were whipping up into the air. I was scared so I went back to the warehouse. But I stopped once, at the fence Vol had pointed out. I had some chalk, and scrawled real big what he had told me. That was all I could do. I didn't understand anything about it. But it made me feel funny when I read it, almost like I didn't even have to know what it meant. I wrote it in a few other places. Pretty soon some other people were scrawling it too. And I thought that was pretty funny. Pretty damn funny."

They had reached the hive houses of the city now. "You're not putting me on?" Jon asked. Surprise sounded in his voice.

"I said you wouldn't believe me." Kino laughed.

"Who said I don't believe you?" Jon's voice gained its evenness once more. "You say it was a man named Catham with a plastic face and a woman called Clea. You're sure you heard the names right?"

"Sure I'm sure," Kino said. "Say, you're not one of the people after Vol, are you?"

"Maybe I am," Jon said.

"Hell," said Kino, "if I'm gonna rat on a friend like that I should've charged you money. What you want him for?"

"For me to know and you to find out," Jon said. "Where do you hang out if I want to talk to you again?"

"Around," Kino said. "Next time, gimme some money for opening my yapper, you hear?"

"Where's around?"

"Well, there's a place that Vol was staying. Old woman runs it, with a bar on the ground floor. She don't hastle about serving people under twenty-one." He gave Jon the location.

"I may see you there," Jon said.

"O.K." said Kino. "And remember about the damn money, huh? It's a hard life, pit-worm."

"Scoot," said Jon.

Kino grinned, and scooted.

CHAPTER FOUR

ALTER had left a message tape at his apartment. As he played it through, her grey eyes blinked pertly, she smiled, and said, "Come and tell me how it went with your father," and clicked off. Jon put one foot on the desk in front of him, switched the re-video from play-back to intra-city, and called the royal palace. The Duchess of Petra's face now looked into his own. She sat back at her desk too, and pushed her red hair from her forehead.

"Want to hear something funny?"

"What, Jon?"

"I found out where Clea and Rolth Catham are."

"Where?"

"With the guy who first said that line we were talking about this afternoon: *You Are Trapped in That Bright Moment Where You Learned Your Doom.* Right?"

The Duchess frowned.

"It was a guy named Vol Nonik, a poet of sorts, also an ex-mali leader." Then he related the story Kino had told him.

"Vol Nonik," mused Petra. "Clea, Catham, and Nonik go off somewhere in a helicopter yesterday morning. You couldn't get any idea what there was between this Nonik fellow and your sister and brother-in-law?''

"A blank," Jon said.

"I'll check in General Records," the Duchess said, "and call you if anything turns up there."

"If you call this evening I'll be over at Alter's."

"Maybe the two of you can wander over to the inn where Nonik was staying and see if you can find anything about him there."

"Good idea," he said.

The night air was warm. The small apartment where the young acrobat had lived since she left the circus was the same one his sister, Clea, had lived in for the years she had tried to shut herself off from the world. Alter, he thought; Alter, who had managed to burst the shrinking globe of the mathematician's retreat and had pried his sister from the cocoon of her guilt back to reality. Now his sister had disappeared again. Jon shook his head as he knocked on Alter's door.

"Hello," she said, opening it to him. "I'm glad you came. Did you find out about Clea from your father?"

He grinned. "You sure ask loaded questions."

The smile turned into apprehension. "Oh, Jon, it did go all right with your father, didn't it? You did speak to him. Was he still very angry?"

"I spoke to him," he said. "It worked out a lot better than I thought it would. I still have a father; and my father still has . . . a son."

"I'm glad," she said, and took his hand and squeezed it. "I think of my aunt, sometimes, not being able to see her, not knowing even if she's alive or not. I know what it must be like for you. Or almost, anyway." They went to the table and Alter sat down. "What about Clea? Where did she go?"

"I only know this much," Jon said. "She and Rolth Catham were married, and then they disappeared."

"She married Catham?" asked Alter in surprise. Then she laughed. "Well, I'm glad of that, too. I guess they were the only people who could really understand each other, anyway. Where did they go?"

"Don't know," said Jon. "But here's something interesting. Remember that line we saw on the fountain this morning?"

Alter nodded.

"The author was a mali poet named Vol Nonik, and the last person to see him saw Clea and Catham taking him off in a helicopter." He gave her the details.

Alter whistled. "That's funny."

"Sure is. Petra said she would check and call if she——"

The video-phone buzzed. Alter answered, and once more that evening Jon saw the Duchess's face. "Jon there?" she asked.

"Right here," he answered from across the room.

"Well, I just made an enemy for life of the night librarian over at Central Records, but I got something on Mr. Nonik."

"Spill."

"What?" asked the Duchess. "Spill what?"

Jon laughed. "Just some gutter slang I'd been remembering. It means go on."

"Oh," said Petra. "Well, first, Nonik was a bright kid in school, though a bit erratic. Bright enough, however, to get a scholarship to the University, where he majored in languages, minored in sociology. Two of his sociology classes were with Rolth Catham.''

''Did they know each other well?'' Jon asked.

''Probably,'' Petra said. ''He was scheduled for Catham's seminar on twentieth-century America, which was an honours seminar restricted to six students personally picked by Catham.''

''You say he was scheduled for it?'' Alter asked. ''Didn't he take it?''

''No.''

''Why not?'' asked Jon.

''He was expelled from the University for 'conduct unbecoming to a student.' It's unspecified exactly what.''

''Probably writing nasty poems about the teachers on the walls of the john.''

''Do they do that at universities too?'' Alter asked.

''At least we know where they know each other from,'' Jon said. ''Now we have to figure out what they have to do with each other.''

''I may even have an answer to that,'' the Duchess said. ''Arkor is checking something for me right now. Oh, here he is.'' She glanced down at something handed to her, then looked up. ''He had a hunch and it paid off,'' she said. ''The week that Nonik was expelled there's a record of Catham making a purchase of a transceivicule.''

''A what?'' asked Alter.

''A transceivicule,'' said Petra. ''It's a small, two-way radio that can be grafted by surgery into the throat. The weekend that Nonik left they both had a pair grafted into them by the University medical department.''

''You mean the two of them have been in radio-contact ever since Nonik was in college.''

"A little over three years," Petra said. "Yes, they have."

"What on earth for?" asked Alter.

The image on the visaphone shrugged. "That I don't know; but as far as the helicopter picking him up off the street, Catham and Clea were probably looking for him and just following the radio signals."

"What about Clea and Nonik?" Jon asked. "Were my sister and Nonik at the University at the same time?"

"Yes, but she was in the graduate department and he was still at grade level. I gather too that she kept pretty tightly to her own department back then. Well, that's all I have."

"That's a lot," Alter said.

"Only it still doesn't tell us why they were together, or where they went. Petra, is there any record at the airport about the 'copter, or for that matter, even anything we could do to stop the enemy—I mean ourselves?"

The Duchess started to say something. Then the firm expression she had held her face in suddenly went. "I . . . I don't know, Jon. I just don't know any more. The council is trying to pretend it isn't happening and is paralysed with panic because they know it is. Perhaps we'll have to go to Telphar ourselves. But short of that, I just don't know."

"We'll find them," Jon said. "If we don't, then Telphar it is."

The Duchess regained her composure. "Try where Nonik lived. Maybe there's some clue there. That's all I can think of now."

"Will do," Jon said. Abruptly the Duchess switched off. Jon turned to Alter. "Ready for a walk?"

"Um-hm."

Jon eased himself up from the chair and frowned as he turned to the acrobat. "She's tired," he said.

Alter nodded. "I know, Jon."

"I guess I would be too if I were trying to run a whole country with a panic-stricken bunch of old men, on one hand, and a seventeen-year-old king who spent the past three years away from court. About all you can really say for him is that he's bright and amenable."

"Let's go to Nonik's inn."

"Come on," said Jon, and they went out.

Night stitched darkly between the roofs. The buildings themselves, as Jon and Alter walked towards the Pot, were lower, closer together, and more dilapidated. They turned down one of the stone alleys that marked the oldest section of the city. Though it was evening, there were more people walking in this part of the city than in the central area.

Alter smiled as they passed two men arguing over a bundle. The package was ill wrapped, and under the street lamp they could see it contained old clothing. "Home again," Alter laughed. "I bet they stole it, and now they can't decide who gets what. The inn must be down this way." They turned another corner. "When I think about all the times I ran these streets, I get positively homesick. I don't know why, though. It was a hungry life, and whenever I was stuck here I couldn't wait to get out with another carnival."

On the corner was a fruit stand under a blue canopy. Lights beneath the awning lit a display of hydroponically grown fruit, and in a glass refrigerator case the plump, shiny aquarium-grown fish lay on glittering ice. The seller, in a white apron, was completing a sale.

Alter glanced to see if he was looking, then snatched a melon. As they turned the next corner, she broke it open and handed half of it to Jon. She bit into the sweet pulp, but Jon held his as they walked.

Finally, he smiled and shook his head.

"What is it?" Alter asked.

"I was just thinking. I spent five years in prison, and I've never stolen anything like food or money in my life. Before I went to prison I had everything I wanted, so that when I got there the idea of taking something never occurred to me. Now the Duchess pays me. And you know something else? When I saw you take that my first reaction was surprise and I guess what you'd call a little moral indignation."

Alter's eyes widened. Then she frowned. "I guess it was a silly thing to do . . . I mean, I was just remembering how we used to swipe fruit when I was little. But you're right, Jon. Stealing is wrong——"

"Wrong or right," Jon said. "I didn't say anything about that."

"But I thought——"

"And the second thing *I* thought was, she comes from the Pot, I come from the hub, and there's a whole set of morals and customs that keeps us apart from one another. And I thought how do you get around all those things, and really touch?"

She started to say something, but stopped, and only watched him.

"Right or wrong," he said. "Hell, I'm a murderer, remember? But how do we touch? I'm a rich man's son, and you're a circus girl from the Pot. Visiting the stage setting for my childhood probably brought all this up. But

I have an answer: we've already touched, in all the things you've taught me, telling me when to put my head back, to tuck my chin, roll. And we can still touch, so simply. Like this''—he took her hand—''and like this.'' He bit into the sweet fruit.

She gave his hand a little squeeze. "Yes. Only about not touching, I know that too. Remember the time we spent on Petra's estate, before we came back here to Toron? I spent so much time being uncomfortable over such silly little things, like which fork to pick up first, when to get up and when to sit down, and who I could scratch in front of, and whom it was worth my life to let a *damn* or a *hell* slip out with. When you're trying to stop a war those are very silly things to think about. But I thought about them. You know I used to think you could just sit around and wait for things to happen, and all you had to worry about was the next meal. But being around you and the Duchess, I guess it taught me this: you have to go out and do and learn; otherwise you spend much too much time being uncomfortable.'' She shrugged. ''That's probably why Tel and I spent so much time together out there. Even though he was from the mainland, he was a lot more like me in that way, we could have run together.'' She fingered her necklace of shells for a moment. ''But he's dead now, killed in the war. So what do I do?''

"Did you love him?'' Jon asked.

Alter let her head drop to the side. ''I liked him a whole lot.'' She glanced back up at Jon. ''But he's dead.''

After a moment Jon asked, ''Then what are you going to do?''

"Learn,'' she said. ''You may have to teach me: call it a mutual exchange.'' They laughed together now.

A fairly solid building stood in the midst of so much sagging clapboard and rusting sheet metal. As they reached the doorway, Alter said, "I hope this trip doesn't turn out to be for——"

As she stepped inside, she stopped.

The woman with the purple birthmark, standing behind the counter, glanced up, then stepped back and opened her mouth.

Alter had grabbed Jon's arm. She let go of it slowly and whispered, "Aunt Rara!"

The woman ran from behind the counter, wiping her hands on her apron. She stopped in the middle of the floor, still open-mouthed, shook her head, then swallowed, and came on again. Alter met her, arms locking about the older woman's shoulders. "Aunt Rara!"

"Oh, Alter! How . . . where . . .?" Then she shook her head again, the expression on her face resolved to smile. But there were tears on her cheeks. "You're back with me," was all she said, the timbre of her voice rough with relief.

The people in the tavern, many of them in military uniform, looked up.

Alter stood back from her aunt. "Aunt Rara, you mean you work in this place?"

"Work in it? I own it. I've got my licence. Really I do."

"Own it?"

"I've been doing all sorts of things and saving all sorts of money, wheedling and conniving here and there. There's very little a practical woman can't do if she sets her mind to it. Oh, Alter, I looked for you, but I couldn't find you!"

"I looked for you too, but Geryn's old place was torn down!"

"I know. For a while I had a job as nurse's aid in General Medical. I searched every circus and carnival that came to Toron."

"I wasn't working until a few months ago."

"Of course! That's when I stopped looking." Again Rara shook her head, blinking away tears. "I'm so glad to see you. So glad!" They embraced again.

"Aunt Rara," Alter said, rubbing her eyes with one knuckle, "I'd like to talk to you about something. Could you help me? I have to find out about somebody who lived here."

"Of course," Rara said. "Of course." Now she saw Jon for the first time. "Young man," she said, "will you watch the place while I go and talk to my niece, for a moment."

"Oh, Aunt Rara," Alter said, remembering herself, "this is Jon Koshar, my friend."

"I'm glad to meet you," Rara said, nodding. "Just watch everybody and make sure nothing cataclysmic happens." She surveyed the figures in the room. "Don't let anyone leave without paying. Though it doesn't look if anyone's going to leave at all." She turned towards the back room, holding Alter by the hand. "Pour yourself a drink if you want." Suddenly she put her hand over her heart and took a breath. "Pour everybody a drink!" And she hurried off, dragging Alter with her.

Still grinning, Jon went to the counter, poured himself a drink, and sat next to a soldier at the bar. The man looked up, nodded vaguely, and then looked down again. His emphatic reaction to Alter's reunion with her aunt made Jon expansive. "You guys seem to be making an evening of it!" he told the soldier. "How're you doing?"

The soldier looked up again. "Rather clumsily," he said. "How'm I doing? You should have asked, 'What am

I doing?' '' He nodded sagely at Jon. "Now that's the question."

"O.K.," Jon said. "What are you doing?"

"I am getting drunk." He picked up his mug of green liquid and ran his finger around the wet ring. It suddenly struck Jon that something was going on in the soldier's mind, and he tried to catch the tone as the soldier went on, "I am making a clumsy attempt to hide, if you will, in a glass." There were a lot of empty mugs in front of him.

"Why?" Jon asked, trying to relate the cynicism to his own good feeling.

The soldier turned so that Jon saw his insignia: a Captain's shield from the Psychological Corps. Since the Moment, many of them had removed their insignia, as had many soldiers discarded their uniforms. "You see," the officer went on a little drunkenly, "I'm one of the ones who knew about the war, who planned it, figured out the best way to make it come off. How do you do, fellow citizen; I'm glad to shake your hand." But he didn't offer his hand and turned back to his drink.

Ordinarily Jon knew better than to try and pry out someone so wrapped in moodiness. But he wasn't in an ordinary mood. "You know——" Jon began.

The psyche officer looked up.

"—I wasn't in the army, but sometimes I have the feeling that perhaps I missed out on something by not being there. If nothing else, I think it's an experience that turns boys into men."

"Yes, I know you do," the psyche officer said shortly.

"The physical discipline, and the experience in action," Jon went on, "even if it was a hypnotic dream, must have meant something, because the death that waited for them was real."

"Look," the psyche officer said, "we did a lot more than plan the combat. We controlled all the propaganda that went to civilians too. I said, 'I know what you think.' "

Jon was surprised. "You don't believe that military discipline can be a good experience?"

"An experience is what you make it," the officer said. "That's real profound, huh? Boys into men? Look at the guys who like the army, or even do well there. Guys who hate the random inconsistency of their parents so much they are willing to give up love to get a father who hands out his orders by a book of rules you can run and check in the library, even if the rule is go out and die. You'll do a lot better if you come to terms with the father you already have than by running off to the state substitute."

Despite drunkenness, the man was maintaining logic, so Jon went on, "But doesn't the army give you a fairly rigorous microcosm to work out certain problems of . . . well, honour and morality, at least for your-self——"

"Sure," drawled the officer, "a microcosm totally safe, completely unreal, free of women and children, where God is the general and the Devil is death, and you're playing for keeps—the excuse for conducting everything with high seriousness. It was all set up to make the most destructive and illogical human actions appear as controlled and non-random as possible. By the time the psycho-economic situation of Toromon had reached the point where 'war was inevitable' we had to have some place for all the sick minds, wounded by just that psycho-economic situation, to fall into. That's the army. But our job was to make the rest of you think it was safe and glorious and good, too. Boys into men? Discipline that isn't self-discipline doesn't mean a thing to a boy. Your hand . . ."

Jon looked down. Whichever way an acrobat turns around a suspended bar, thumbs lead and fingers follow; the reverse grip that must be second nature had got Jon in the habit of laying his hands before him palms up. The calluses from the mine had come back quickly on the bar.

". . . those hands can move and make and do. You talk like an intelligent man, so you probably do what you do well. When you learned to do whatever made those calluses that was discipline. Can you build, can you follow the rules of some craft, can you submit those hands to order, working along with someone else, or alone? I don't know what you do, but I know that in educating those hands you've had more discipline than any dozen men who know only how to kill in a dream. What you already have in those hands, we had to lie ourselves blue to make you *think* the army could give you. We had it so finely planned! The novels, the stories, the articles, all answering emphatically 'Yes!" to the questions you've just asked. The psyche corps didn't write them, either.

"We'd done our propaganda job already, laid the grounding for all the uncertain and doubting intellectuals to do the rest; 'Yes, yes! The war is a real and valid experience,' because they, among you all, might have doubted enough to figure out it was a fake. Make you into a man? Look at them, why don't you? Just look." He gestured towards the other soldiers in the tavern.

One was asleep across the table in the corner. Two more were beginning to argue near the door, while a fourth looked on anxiously, expecting a fight. A fifth laughed hysterically at something the brown-haired girl with him said, leaned back in his chair, holding his stomach, and fell over backwards. Now the girl began to laugh.

The psychologist wavered on his stool and turned back to the bar. "Or look at me," he said. He talked into the glass before him. "Look at me."

"You think the whole thing, without any redemption, was meaningless?" Jon asked. His thoughts went to Tel, who was dead, Alter's friend, Tel. "For all of them, it meant nothing?"

The psychologist shook his head slowly. "You don't see. You just don't see. You knew someone who went up in cinders inside one of those death-tanks, didn't you. You want like hell to make it mean something. But I knew a lot of guys who died. I trained them. There's not one who wouldn't have become a lot more of a man doing whatever you did to get those hands. I don't care what it is." The officer made a face. "Because life . . . living"—he reached out with his finger and flipped a coin on the counter against the square of coins that was his change: two other coins shot from the far side of the matrix of metal discs—"is like that. The enemy isn't always somebody you can shoot at over a gravel bag. There isn't always somebody to tell you when to shoot and when to cease fire. The women and children haven't been left conveniently behind, and because they haven't, you're forced to look at them and see that they have their problems, which look surprisingly like your own—a hard fact for too many 'mature' men to accept. The army is just too easy and too simple: fight to the death for the cause is just." The officer looked at Jon. "You knew somebody who got burned. Well, compared with what you have to live for, he didn't die for a damned thing." He paused. "That's hard to take."

"This is how you take it?" Jon asked. Once out, the words sounded cruel, but he had said them with wonder, a beginning of understanding.

The psyche officer chuckled. "Yeah," he said. "Like this." The chuckle passed away like gravel from a roof. Now he frowned and shook his head. "They don't hate me. You know, they still don't hate me. They come in here, drink with me, razz me about not having seen real combat, with all sorts of goodwill, even though they know I was one of the ones responsible. Oh, we did our work so well, well, well. It's easier for them, still, to go along with the feelings we tried so hard to instil. But I'm a psychologist, see, so I know exactly why I'm sitting here getting drunk. I know all that's going on in my mind, making me do it. And I know why I went and got drunk last night. And I know why I got drunk the night before that. I know, they know, and it doesn't help a damn bit."

Alter and her aunt came from the back room, and Jon turned on the stool.

"Well, here we are," Rara said, wiping her eyes on her apron. "Now you come back soon," she said to her niece. "Your old aunt is a respectable woman now."

"I will," Alter said, and hugged her. She turned to Jon and took his hand.

"Sure the two of you wouldn't like something to eat?" asked Rara, "or maybe just to stay and talk a little while?"

"That's all right," Alter said. "But we can't now. We'll come back soon."

"Very soon," Rara said. "Please make it very soon."

They walked from the inn slowly. "Did you find anything about Nonik?"

"Um-hm," she nodded. In her hand was a folded

packet of paper. "Some of his poems. They were left in his room after . . ." She shuddered and handed them to Jon.

"What did your aunt want to talk to you about?" he asked.

She was silent a moment. "She wanted me to stay there with her, and live there."

Jon nodded.

"The whole thing caught me when I wasn't looking. I even think I might have liked to. But I've got my own apartment, and I'm just used to being on my own." She brushed her white hair from the back of her neck. "At the same time I realized how much I loved her."

"You know," Jon said, "I guess I have to be hit over the head with something before it takes."

"How do you mean."

"I was thinking about what I said to you about customs and morals keeping people apart, making them different from one another. People are so much more alike than different. So much more."

Slowly they walked from the city's rim, through the pithy strictures of the night, back together to look at the poems.

CHAPTER FIVE

Take rage and twist it through loops of violence; with the circle ring the lipped pit of the brain; set brain in bone, and tell man in the dark he is alone.

Blue water runnelled the cellar floor, and from the

corner came the smell of damp fish-sacks. Jeof squatted on a barrel. He turned his hands over in his lap, closing and opening the fingers, a gesture in which he could let fragments of the isolate terror. His perception dim, his breathing slow, he sat in the dark as he had for the last hour and a half, not so much thinking as allowing pictures to form in his mind: a girl's face, eyes closed, a line of blood from her mouth, thin as a red pencil mark; a body falling on the wharf as sirens filed at the darkness; a store window shattering brightly before his jutting fist in moonlight. That time his arm had been cut. He still had the scar. He touched the welt under the hair of his forearm. Here, he thought, I can sit quietly within this rage and be alone. The loneliness was painful, but he accepted it because he could think of no other way to be. He closed his fingers again, trying to catch the terror. Perhaps some day he would stop trying. But that was a long time away.

Doctor your wounds with evil. Leave your blood over the wharf cobbles webbed with mud. The ambient heart stalks from the sea into the city's mystery.

Renna's mother watched her living-room door close as the police officer went out, and thought, My eyes will explode, perhaps I shall scream. Maybe the plaster will begin to crack and shatter up the walls. She waited. Nothing happened, so she sucked in a breath and heard herself sob. She turned, thinking, A coin dropped into deep water, spinning as it falls.

Then she went to the visaphone and dialled Dr. Wental. He was the only doctor in the building, and even as she finished dialing and the piercing buzz began, she wondered. What am I calling a doctor for? What in the world am I calling a doctor for!

Dr. Wental's face focused. "Yes?"

And something inside her tore apart and she was crying,

"Dr. Wental, for the love of . . . help me . . . she's dead, my daughter, Renna, she's been . . . Oh, she's dead . . ." The half phrases stumbled from her tongue. Something burned her lips, her cheeks, seared her eyes blind until only tears could wash back sight.

"You're the woman who lives on the second floor?"

"Yes, I . . . yes . . ."

She wondered what her face looked like. But the doctor frowned a moment and then said, "I'll be right down," and switched off. Time passed. Time is always passing, she thought. Where am I going in all this passing time? There was a knock on the door.

Hysterically calm she went to open it, and the doctor stepped inside.

"I'm sorry," she said. "I'm so sorry. I didn't mean to disturb you, Doctor. There's nothing you can do, I mean for me. There's nothing . . . why did I get you all the way down here? . . ." She shook her head.

"Don't bother to apologize," Dr. Wental said. "I quite understand."

"The officer was just here. He told me. They couldn't identify her till now from her retina pattern because her eyes were all . . ."

"Perhaps I can give you a sedative."

"No," she said. "No I don't want a sedative. I didn't mean to call you down here . . . I mean . . ." Then the embarrassments she had been mouthing for nearly a minute became real. "Oh, Dr. Wental, I just wanted to talk to somebody. I thought of a doctor first, I don't know why. But I just wanted to talk."

"Are you sure you don't want a sedative?"

"Oh, no," she said again. "Here, let me get us both a drink."

"Well"—he paused—"well, all right."

She went to the cupboard and got out glasses and the green bottle. Just the movement of walking over the floor, the fall of her wrist as she turned the knob, the smooth pressure of glass against thumb and forefinger brought back the physical part of her she had forgotten. She moved quickly into the kitchenette and pushed the wall treadle with her foot. The table swung out, and she set the glasses and bottle down on the surface of chipped blue stone.

"Let me," said Dr. Wental, pulling up a chair for her. As she sat down, he stepped around the table, opened the bottle, and poured out the drinks. When she picked up hers he seated himself, finished his in one gulp, and poured himself another, but with such self-assurance that she didn't even think about it.

She looked at the green liquid shivering in the wide mouth of her glass, and said, "Dr. Wental, I feel so alone. I want to run some place, crawl under something, be told what to do. When my own parents died I didn't feel anything like this . . ."

"They say that the death of a child," began the doctor, and finished the statement with a nod. Had he taken a third drink?

"I love her so much, spoil her, I suppose. I sent her to parties, bought her clothes . . . oh, the clothes. I bought her so many clothes," and she felt something inside her begin to tear again. Catching at the edges, she continued, "All parents live through their children, Doctor. It isn't wrong. It isn't wrong, is it?" She ran her hand over her hair, and the scarf caught in her fingers. When she brought it before her the silken green with its design of blue and red seaweed was so vivid, and the loose skin of her hand so terribly grey.

When she looked up the doctor was pouring himself still

another glass. He smiled apologetically: "I guess I'm depleting your store here a bit. Forgive me."

"Oh, that's all right," she replied vaguely. "I hardly ever use it. Go ahead, please."

"Thank you."

"I feel like I have to give something to somebody, do something for somebody, make believe I'm"—she paused—"I was going to say alive." She moved the glass back and forth in front of her. The light from the wall fixture struck through the green and fell shimmering on the blue stone. "Make believe I'm alive," she repeated.

"Did you start to say, 'Make believe she's alive'?" the doctor suggested.

She shook her head. "No. No, I know what I said." She looked up. "I think I will take the sedative. I really don't want anything to drink."

"Very well."

"I'll be all right now. Thank you for coming, for letting me feel for a little while that I wasn't alone. But there's . . . nothing I can do about it, is there?"

"There's nothing you can do about your daughter," Dr. Wental said.

"That's what I meant." She stood up from the table. "I'll take your sedative and rest now."

The doctor nodded and started to rise.

She frowned. "Are you all right, Doctor?" He had grabbed the edge of the table.

He smiled again. "Perhaps I depleted your store a little too much." He rose to his full height and stepped unsteadily from the table.

In the living-room he searched in his bag a long time for the amber glass pill bottle. 'I'll leave one . . . two"—he swayed, and the hem of his tan jacket shook against his thigh—"two of these with you. Take one, at first, and if you need more, to settle you, take the other one." He handed her the pills on a pad of surgical gauze.

She followed him to the door and opened it for him. As he stepped into the hall he seized the door jamb, as before he had caught himself on the table edge. She frowned; then, trying to turn her own concern into a joke, she laughed, "You'd better not tell your wife how much you've had down here. You wouldn't want your wife to know."

She saw his back stiffen under the tan cloth. Slowly he turned back. "I suppose I ought to inform you," he announced thickly, "that I gave you those sedatives illegally. As for my wife, she won't know, because she doesn't live with me any more."

She looked surprised.

"A week ago I was charged and convicted of malpractice. Tampering with drugs—somebody died. Well, my wife does know, and she left me. So I really don't have to bother about keeping anything from her any more."

He turned again and moved off unsteadily down the hall. Bewildered, she stepped back into the empty apartment.

The image of your eye cased in a jewel. Outside the solitary rooms of sleep observes the acrobat, the thief, the fool, the workings of ambition, death, and grief. Magnificent and isolate, then, dream.

The King watched his cousin by the window, absently fingering a smokey stone set in a silver chain around her neck. Petra let the curtain fall back across the lights of the city and turned to him. Her red hair, loosed from the golden comb shaped like crab claws, fanned across her shoulder. "What is it, Petra?" he asked.

"What is what, my King?"

"Please, Petra," he said, "don't pretend to be formal. Just be my cousin as you used to be, when you would tell me stories."

The Duchess smiled and shook her head. "Let, I'm running out of stories to tell."

"Then tell me the truth. What's bothering you?"

"I told you about the 'enemy' going wild," she said, walking to the couch and sinking down. "You've been at the council meetings. You've done a splendid job too. You've argued down ministers calmly whom I would have ended up screaming at. Let——"

"——while you sat beside me," he went on for her, "as my adviser. I wish they allowed you to speak at official meetings, Petra. All the calm arguing I do is what you've gone over with me beforehand. I can see you aching to speak. That's probably what's rubbed your nerves so raw."

She laughed. "You're right about the nerves. But it's just as well you do all the talking at the council meetings. You're a remarkably articulate boy."

"But I am a boy, only seventeen, and I haven't forgotten it. Neither has the council. Sometimes I can almost hear you thinking, 'If protocol only allowed me to say the same thing . . .' " He sighed. "But that's responsible for only half. What about the other half?"

Petra was silent a moment. "Sometimes I think you learned to read minds too in the years you spent among the forest guards."

"I learned to observe carefully," he said. "And I've watched you. Now will you tell me?" His voice was both calm and imperative, the voice through which she had made what little progress she had with the council.

She rose again and crossed to the window, and once more pushed back the brocade drape. A breeze waved her blue robes. Let watched half expressions seat themselves in the strong lineaments. "It's doubt, Let. A great and serious doubt."

"What do you doubt, Petra?"

"I doubt you. I doubt me." With her free hand she motioned through the open window towards the pattern of lights on the darkness. "This island, this empire, spread around us; we are responsible for it. And I doubt us, deeply, Let, deeply." Again she let the drape swing back.

"How do you doubt, Petra?"

He watched her breathe in, then hold the air as if afraid to release it. "Let," she said at last, "years ago I conceived a plan, before the war was even declared, that I thought might save Toromon. I love Toromon, Let, her ships, her farms, her factories, her forests . . . I knew she was weak. And the plan was to save her strength, and do whatever I could to ease the economic trauma Toromon was passing through by guiding the reins of the council whenever I could. But primarily my hope was in you, getting you away from your mother and your brother, and then restoring you to the throne. I thought Toromon would need a strong and articulate king. The training you received in the forest was all that I could have hoped. Yet now I doubt the whole plan, my part in it, and yours."

"I still don't quite——"

She turned from the window a last time. "The aristocracy of Toromon is just not capable of holding the country together. It's too old, too tired, too tied up with the council to make the sweeping changes that might save us; but it's too powerful to die. Maybe I shouldn't have spent my efforts trying quietly to control the country. Maybe I should have gone about the whole thing completely differently. Perhaps the answer was to smash the existing government and to let a new, vigorous one grow out of whatever was left healthy in Toromon. Maybe I should have become a mali and destroyed for the destruction's sake. There's so much more evil than good in the whole system. Have I been trying to keep alive something that would have been better dead a long time ago? Let, I doubt deeply how right I was. And if I *have* done wrong, then I have done more wrong than anyone for over five hundred years." She sat down on the cushions, lifting her long fingers to her neck, bringing them around to rub away the fatigue that had gathered there from holding her regal head so high.

"It is a great responsibility, Petra," the young King said emptily.

She leaned her head back. When she looked up again he saw tears banked on her lower lids. "Let, I feel so alone," she said softly, blinked, and the tears were on her cheek.

"Petra." The King leaned forward from his chair, urgency in his voice. "Petra?"

"Yes?"

"If you could do anything in the world you wanted to do, what would it be—I mean something that had nothing to do with Toromon?"

"I don't know," she said. "Something that has nothing to do with Toromon—it's been a long time since I could want anything like that. What do you want, my King?"

"Petra, I feel alone too."

She tilted her head to the side. "Yes. You must. This is lonely work."

"It is." He nodded. "Everyone I know well is in the forest. Here, you're my only friend. But when I feel very bad, sometimes I think about what I would do if . . . and I think some day I'll do it. Then I feel better."

"What do you want to do?" She smiled.

"It should be different for each person," he explained, "but——"

"But tell me."

Again the King leaned forward, his hands joined tightly in front of him. Already, she saw, they were beginning to lost some of the rich colouring they had gained during his exile to the mainland forest. "I remember, from a long time ago, even before I was taken to the mainland, I remember a boy—I don't recall exactly how I knew him, but he was from the coast and he was a fisherman's son. He told me all about working on the boats, rocks of all different colours, and in the morning, he said, you can see the sun come up like a burning blister on the water. He told me about fishing too. I'd like to work on a boat, Petra. Oh, not be carried from place to place with other people turning the wheel. I want to be in control, going where I want to go, smacking down the waves as they come up to me, and as they rise about me, I cut through." He paused a moment, blue eyes glowing. The yellow hair, run with paler streaks from the bleaching mainland sun, was again darkening to gold. "I'm alone," he said, "like you, Petra. But when I feel it very strongly I think: Some day, like that boy—whoever he was—I'll ride on a boat, and steer it into the sea. It helps."

"Good," she said. For the third time she went to the window and pushed back the curtain. This time, however she motioned to him. "Come stand with me, my King." Let rose and walked to her side. "Toromon," she said, and he nodded, gazing across the lights of the city to the midnight sea.

"And we are in the centre," he said, "both alone."
*Order these desperate strokes to single lines, separate
and tangible, beautiful and real; fish-bones throw their
shadows on the wall, portending the ideal.*

Arkor stood in the laboratory tower in the west wing of
the royal palace of Toron. At the end of the metal band was
a crystal sphere, fifteen feet in diameter, which hovered
above the receiving platform. A dozen small tetron units
of varying sizes sat about the room. The viewing screens
were dead. On a control panel by one ornate window a
bank of forty-nine scarlet-knobbed switches pointed to
off. Arkor was walking slowly across the catwalk above
the stage. He reached the balcony and paused before the
night. A breeze combed through his hair.

He glanced back into the room. Across the catwalks,
the platform, and the sphere fell the long shadows from the
super-structure of conversion equipment that had turned
the transit-ribbon into a matter projector for use in the war.
It had never been used. He looked out again into the city.

Normally the giant's telepathic receptivity was only a
few hundred feet, but recently he had found his range
expanding, sometimes for an hour or more, to cover
miles. As he stepped on to the balcony, he felt the subsen-
sory tingling that announced one of these attacks. Suddenly the city, as though a veil were pulled away, was
revealed to him as a vast matrix of minds, clashing, jarring
one another, yet each isolate. I am alone, he thought,
adding the millionth repeat to a million-fold echo. The few
other telepaths in the city, as well as the non-telepathic
guards, flashed on the web of dimmer minds. But even
trying to contact them was at best like touching through
glass. There was only the image, without warmth or
texture. Isolate, he thought, letting the pattern fill him,

alone in the palace tower, in the tower of my own perceptions, as a brute neanderthal guilty at the City's rim, as
King and Duchess beside me, minds circled and alone,
standing together as the drunken doctor and grieving
mother part a mile away.

Somewhere a man and woman sat—Jon and Alter, but
he identified them only after he picked them out—together
in a room, shoulder to shoulder, heads bent together,
reading a poem from a crumpled paper, now stopping to
ask each other what this line meant, now going back to
look at another page. The patterns growing in their minds
were not the same, but as they tried to explain what they
thought to each other, or bent to read or reread the lines,
the images the poem made upon their thoughts were like
flames dancing orderly about one another, contrasting or
similar, still a single experience, an awareness of unity,
unaware of their isolation. Delusion? thought Arkor. No.
The now brittle, now flexible, bending and quivering
lights danced orderly together. Arkor smiled, alone as the
two bent closer to the paper. Jon held the page, while Alter
unfolded a corner that had been bent down across the last
stanza:

*Bring me to a city gold and grey where the human and
the wild can mesh, not where I am gutter-bound by fish-
bones.*

CHAPTER SIX

"ALL right," Alter said. "You teach me now." She
opened the box where she kept her small collection. "It's
not much, but it's all I've got. What should I wear?"

Jon glanced over the green lining where the few pins, brooches, and necklaces lay. "First of all, as little as possible." He grinned. "It's a formal affair of state, and Toromon is an empire bound up with the sea. That means all your jewellery should take its pattern and substance from the ocean. At a less formal affair you could get away with some of the floral designs. But since it's high state, I'd say just the shell necklace you wear most of the time anyway; then the pearl earrings and the pearl buckle. That'll do it."

She picked them from the box and went to the chair where the beige silk gown lay. "I just can't get over this. It's beautiful. I'll never be able to thank Petra for having it made for me. Imagine wearing a dress that probably cost half a year's circus salary." She held it up in one hand and fanned out the panels with the other. Then she frowned. "What're these?"

"Where?"

"Here." She had a look of disappointment.

"Pockets," said Jon, surprised at her reaction.

"Really fine women's clothing doesn't have pockets!"

"Huh?" Then he laughed.

"What's so funny? Here I thought this was a——"

"Look," Jon said, "if you're going to make your entrance into society you might as well do it all the way and know what you're doing."

Her frown grew puzzled.

"I wasn't born into the aristocracy, but grew up next to it, so I can give you some insights into its working that Petra might never think of mentioning. Toromon's aristocracy can be an amazingly functional group of people; at least they were when they were pirates five hundred years ago. And they have always had pockets, though after a while they didn't advertise them. The pockets in that dress are behind a fold, and no one will know you have them unless you walk around with your hands in them. Now the people who make what you call expensive clothes for women—the ones in the downtown dress shops—imitate what they think they see: they equate aristocratic with decorative, useless, unfunctional. Hence, no pockets. This dress was probably made by the Duchess's personal dress-maker, and if the dresses you've seen cost half a year's salary this is more like five or six years' pay." Alter's puzzled expression became delighted surprise. "That's what comes of not having any formal balls out at Petra's estate: you have to wait until you get here to pick that up." He sat down on the couch. "It surprises me the things I remember."

"I'm glad you do," Alter said. "At least I feel I've got some chance of getting through the evening without choking on my ankle. Now you won't let me say the wrong thing!" She seized his wrist. "And if I pick up something in the wrong hand you'll kick me quietly on the shin."

"Did you ever let me fall off the high bar onto my head?"

"Imagine," exclaimed Alter, "and I can't, really —me, even thinking about things like this, a ball at the palace! I'm not supposed to care about silly things like that. But, oh, I do, I do, I do."

"Be yourself," Jon laughed, squeezing her hand. "Keep your conversation light, and remember, the idea is more important than the action to these people. Be gracious; your duty is to take the initiative in gentleness. Speak softly, move slowly, try and spend at least five times as much of your energy listening as talking."

"Oh . . ." breathed Alter. "Do you think I'll be all right?"

Jon smiled. "Hurry up, get dressed."

The spreading windows rose about the hall; stars shone through the upper panes from the clear night. The musicians wove the old melodies with their polished shells, and with the help of a theremin, opened the ball with the familiar anthems of Toromon. "Mr. Quelor Da and party," announced the loud-speaker. Jon glanced at the entrance as the brightly dressed figures, miniatured by the distance of the palace ballroom, descended from the arched entrance. He pushed back his black cloak and thought, How familiar all this is. But so much else was familiar as well. He recalled swinging the mali tongue in the mines—familiar, as the turn and fall of the dances of royalty, the carriage and etiquette of a ball. Glancing at his tall reflection in one of the mirrored walls, he recalled the boy he had been at eighteen. A bit of that was still there—a familiar energy behind the deepened expression, the gaunter face. He smiled, then turned to the dais where the King and the Duchess were receiving.

Jon touched Alter's shoulder, and she turned, silver brows vaulting above large blue eyes. "I think they have a moment." He took her arm. They made their way across the floor to the emerald-clad Duchess. The King's royal white dazzled against the remaining tan from the forest. The pale streaks over his hair were near Alter's semi-albino tresses. Almost, thought Jon, as though they were from the same family. The Duchess held out her hand in greeting. "Jon, Alter," she said warmly. "Here you are! My King? You've all met briefly before."

"Jon I remember well. But"—the King turned to Alter—"it's been a while since I've seen you this close. I've only watched you glittering in the air at the circus, since you kidnapped me."

"It's good to see you back at the palace, my King," Alter said.

"It's boring here," the King said, confidentially. "But you give me something beautiful to contemplate."

"Oh, thank you . . . my King!"

"Do you like the party, Alter?" asked the Duchess.

"It's just . . . beautiful, Your Grace!"

The Duchess bent slightly towards her. "Petra, as usual."

Alter flushed a trifle, and said, "Oh, and Petra, the dress is lovely."

"You double its loveliness."

"Petra, just what is the purpose of this ball?" Jon asked while Alter beamed.

The Duchess's voice lowered. "Primarily to feel out what we can get by way of financial aid from whomever we can. It hasn't changed that much. The war's end has left us in quite a bind."

"Especially since it hasn't really ended," commented Jon.

Petra sighed. "But we must appear as though it has."

Jon thought back to the last ball he had attended at the palace.

"Petra, shall I open the dancing?" asked the King.

She looked over the guests, then nodded.

King Let offered his arm to Alter. "Do you mind dancing with a lame man, to open the ball?"

"My King . . ." Alter said, and glanced at Jon, who nodded gently to her. "Of course I wouldn't mind. Thank you." And she moved off at his side.

Jon and the Duchess watched as, beige and white, the youngsters reached the musicians. "The limp," Jon said, "it's almost gone."

"He tried hard to hide it," said Petra. "When he dances, hardly anyone will notice—because he is King."

The bitterness that momentarily filled her voice surprised him.

"Alter will notice," Jon said. "Her body's a trained, sensitive instrument."

Music began, and the turning figures of the acrobat and the royal youth opened a path through the other guests, who, at the musical signal, themselves broke into bright whirling couples over the white tile floor. The Duchess's eyes, however, were down. When they did look up Jon saw they were bright. "We are disguising Toromon's wounds well this evening," she said softly.

He watched the figures of the dance bloom like a flower. Then the music ended, and petals drifted back to the edge of the floor.

"How did we look?" demanded Let, flushed and a bit breathless, when he and Alter reached the dais.

"Charming," said the Duchess.

People had again come over for the interminable introductions, and Alter stepped quickly to Jon's side. "We'll go now, Petra. I hope it goes well."

"Thank you, Jon."

"Good evening, my King."

"Good evening. We'll dance once more before the evening's over, Alter."

"Oh, yes, my King."

Jon and Alter left the dais and strolled over the floor. "How is it to dance with a king?" asked Jon.

Her hand was on his arm, and now she squeezed gently. "He's sweet. But I had more fun practising with you this afternoon."

"Dance with me now, then," he said, as the music for the partner-changing dance began. She came into his encircling arm, her right hand resting, small—and warm—on his left, the tip of her pinky just pressing the knuckle of his index finger.

"Don't go too far away from me," she whispered. Gowns rustled about them. "I want to be able to get back to you in a hurry."

Turn, dip, separate, join again; through the recalled steps her smile was brilliant. The music rose, she turned away from him, and a girl in blue replaced her in his arms. He nodded graciously and began the figure of the dance again, glancing once at Alter: her new partner was a middle-aged man with short brown hair and heavy lips and whose chest bore the royal insignia of the house of B'rond. Jon exchanged a few civilities with his partner, the music rose again and a moment later Alter whirled back to him.

"Who were you dancing with?"

"Some industrialist's daughter. Her father's in transport; one of the Tildons."

"And who was I dancing with?"

"Count B'rond."

"Do you realize in those two minutes he said I was beautiful, he must see me again, and that I was the most graceful person at the ball, and he would be waiting for me at sunrise at the castle entrance."

"He and his seven wives?" Jon asked. "At least he had had seven before I went to the mines. I think he killed a couple of them, though—accidentally of course."

"That's him?" exclaimed Alter. "Wasn't there some scandal a few years ago, during that exposé of the aristocracy? It was swallowed up with all the business over the emigration from the mainland. They kept talking about some B'rond."

Jon nodded. "Apparently hasn't changed his habits much, either."

Alter pulled her shoulders in and shivered.

"The blue blood of Toromon isn't in all that hot shape. You remember King Uske. And finally the Queen Mother had to be put away. Both of them were batty. Petra's an exception."

"I guess so," Alter said, moving away to the music, coming back, then whirling off. Jon turned to receive his next partner as Alter's beige silk opened like a whispering rose.

Then the windows in the west wall went white: light like swords leapt across the floor. Women cried out; men stepped backwards, throwing their arms over their faces. The shells ceased sounding and the theremin squacked. A moment later thunderous rumbling replaced the music, growing, then fading, as darkness filled the high, coffin-shaped windows once more.

Jon was the first to run forward. Alter was beside him. After them, the others ran to see.

Jon reached the middle window and pushed away the heavy edging. Alter's shoulder jostled against his as others rushed against her.

Far among the city's towers flames flicked through the ruptured skyline.

"What in the world do you . . .?"

"It's the General Medical building . . .!"

"No, no, it couldn't be. Isn't that over . . .?"

"They've bombed the General Medical building! Can't you see! That's where the General Medical building used to be!"

Jon pushed his way back through the crowd. Alter, her skirts held to her legs, pressed after him. "Jon, was it the General Medical?" He nodded shortly to her over his shoulder.

81

Petra intercepted them from another window. "Jon!" Reaching him, she caught his arm. "You saw that!" She shook her head, like a confused beast, red hair leaping sideways, brighter than the flames across the night. "There's no time, Jon. You've got to go to Telphar. That's the only thing left. I would go with you, but somebody must stay to help Let hold the city together. Alter, will you go with him?"

Amazed, she nodded.

"If you can stop this enemy, stop it. If you can find out how it might be stopped, tell me and I'll stop it. Jon, even the records have ceased coming in. The military is threatening to withdraw."

"Can we take Arkor?" Jon asked. "Maybe we can use him?"

Petra hesitated, her white teeth catching her lower lip as she dropped her head in thought. It raised quickly. "No. I can't send him with you. I haven't wanted to, but I may have to use his powers to pry things out of the council. More attacks like this and we'll have to evacuate the city. I can't let the whole population risk being blown to bits. The council is panic-stricken already, and nothing will get done unless I use every method available."

"All right," Jon said, pulling in a breath. About them the ballroom was frantic. "We'll leave now."

"Goodbye, Petra," Alter said.

The Duchess took her hand with sudden urgency. "Goodbye," she said quietly, "and good luck."

At the arched doorway Alter, catching up to Jon, said, "The General Medical building, Jon. Won't that mean——?"

The conversation in the room was rising towards hysteria.

"—It'll mean that the major source of medical supplies for the city is cut off. Let's just hope there isn't a plague before they get it operating again."

The industrialist's daughter in blue had been accosted by Alter's ex-partner, Count B'rond. "It's so terrifying," she moaned. "It reminds me of something I saw a little girl scribbling on a wall this afternoon, something about being trapped at a bright moment . . . trapped——" The lower voice of the count interrupted as he leaned towards her: "You are still the most beautiful woman I have seen during the whole evening." His gloved hand was a moth on her shoulder. "Will you let me see you again?"

Jon and Alter gained the door and went first to the Duchess's suite. Arkor opened the door for them.

"Yes, I know what's happened," he said.

"Then what's the best way to get to Telphar?" Jon dropped his black cloak at the feet of the chair.

"The transit-ribbon's out of commission, at least from this end. That conversion nonsense has left this side useless for sending." From a closet, while he talked, he took two ordinary sets of clothing and handed them out. "There's nothing you'll need I can't give you here, is there?"

"I don't think so," Alter said, reaching into the silken folds of her skirt. "This is all I'd want to take, and I brought them along." She drew out a sheaf of papers.

"Nonik's poems?" Jon pulled off first one openwork boot and then the other. "Reading matter for when things get dull?"

Alter reached behind her back, snapped open a snap, and the dress was a ring of silk about her. She stepped out, stepped into the green tunic, and belted it about her waist with a leather belt. "I'd better leave these." She removed the pearl earrings, started to take off the shell necklace, then bit her lip, shrugged. "I'll wear this." Arkor handed them sandals and they began to lace them up.

Jon closed the top buckle around his shin, and stuck the poems in his shirt pocket, before pushing his arms down the loose three-quarter sleeves. "I'll hold these for you."

"I miss my pockets," Alter laughed.

The video-phone buzzed and the Duchess announced, "All the royal yachts are out. Two reservations are waiting for you on a tetron-tramp at the pier."

They left the Duchess's suite moments later.

As they rushed from the palace on foot open-topped transports carried the more elegant attendants off through the streets. Shoulder to shoulder against the indifferent night, they made their way towards the city's rim.

CHAPTER SEVEN

A SIREN gnawed at the dark. A water main had broken and the street was covered with a black, glittering rush. Orange scimitars from reflected flames streets away flashed in the ripples over the curb.

A white figure staggered across the pavement, whirling absurdly, the soaked hem of the large cloth flapping on her legs. The light struck something shiny and askew on her white, ropey hair. As she tottered to the street lamp it was revealed as a strip of tin, ripped edge-ragged from a can and bent in a circle. She turned and called into the alley: splashes followed her into the light.

Several men and women came along hesitantly, blinking, shuffling, flapping through the water. One youngster, whose hair fell into his face, had, stencilled over his pyjama chest: WARD 739. Aimless crying came from his open mouth. With grubby fingers he kept twisting his right ear.

Something struggled among them. They crowded about an odd duo: one beefy man in soaked pyjama pants had a hammerlock on a frailer figure in white. This white was not a hastily issued nightgown or abruptly snatched sheet, but a short-sleeved, doctor's uniform. It was wet and wrinkled now. The man's arms were tied behind his back and his squinting attested to a pair of lost glasses. His captor, chuckling, held him by the shoulder and whammed the back of his head with the ham of his hand. The bound figure collapsed to one knee on the streaming pavement. "Will you please . . . ?" he began, raising his head, tendons taut in his brown neck, to watch the tall woman. "Look, you don't realize you're not well, none of you. . . . Just let me take you back to . . ."

The tall woman had begun searching the folds of her bedsheet cloak. In frustration she cried out, "Oh, keep him quiet I tell you!" The beefy man flung his foot like a club into the doctor's back and laughed when he splashed forward. Then he hoisted him back up.

"I can't find it!" screeched the woman. Her face went white, then red. "Oh, I can't find it! Who has stolen it? Will nobody answer me! Don't you know who I am! How dare you treat me like this! Haven't you any respect!"

Despair, like the chill water, gushed over the kneeling physician. "Help!" he cried into the darkness. "Help me!" His cry, directed at no one particular, threatened no one, and his persecutor only tilted his broad head curiously to watch him howl. He laughed again and began to chew at the nub of his thumb nail.

Then from the alley splashed a man in green slicker and rubber boots. "Hey, come on," he ordered indignantly, "we're trying to keep this area evacuated till we get the water main fixed. Now clear out and stay away from the flooded area." The officer cursed, coughed, and flung the rubberized cloak back over his shoulder. "Hurry up before I run you in!"

"They've taken it away from me again!" screamed the woman, pawing at her sheet. "I can't find it! They've stolen it again! Oh, why won't they give it back!"

"Help me, *please*," cried the kneeling man.

The youngster with the hair over his face and WARD 739 over his chest sobbed and twisted his ear.

The officer came up short. "What are you, some sort of nuts?"

A young woman broke towards him, a pigeon gurgle falling from her pale mouth. When she passed beneath the street lamp the officer saw she would have been pretty had her eyes not been streaked like a puppy's. Cooing, she embraced him, rubbed her head against his wet slicker.

"Hey, what the hell do you think you're——"

The tall woman whirled on him. "Young man, do you know who you are talking to?"

"The Queen of Sheba for all I know! I was telling her to get——" He staggered as the young woman settled herself from him like a pendulum.

"The Queen!—The Queen? Do you *know* who I am?" demanded the woman again. "Oh, keep him quiet, will you!" She began clutching at her sheet once more.

The officer was still trying to loose the girl hanging from his neck when he heard a giggle in his left ear. He turned, more from instinct than interest, and saw the full lips with the rim of pink tongue pressing between them, the puffy lids of the dark-brown eyes, hair rough and yellow as hemp on the wide skull, the same coarse hair on the wider chest, tufting the thick collarbone——

—The beefy man smashed in the side of the officer's face with his fist; then he hit the officer on the neck with the edge of his hand.

"They stole it," cried the tall woman as the officer sagged out of the girl's arms.

"You . . . you don't know what you're *doing!*" cried the doctor. He was nearly on his feet. "Will you please, will you *please* let me take you some place where they can help you. Just listen to me, just follow me to . . ."

"*Will* you keep him quiet?" demanded the tall woman. "How do you ever expect me to find it!"

Smiling, the beefy man dragged the inert officer across the pavement. His bare feet splashed up water like flat stones. When he reached the doctor he tilted his head, blinked like a puzzled monkey, then kicked the man's feet from under him so that he flopped onto the pavement again, called out in pain and surprise.

"Quiet!" screamed the woman, shaking the wet cloth away from her arms and whirling beneath the lamp.

The beefy man kneeled in the water, clamped his fingers over the necks of both conscious and unconscious men, lifted them and looked from face to face, one limp and bleeding, the other contorted and gasping. He licked his lower lip, his upper one. Then he pushed both faces into the water and held them there.

The doctor struggled a while.

Sobbing, the youngster with the long hair bent over the glistening rubber back and tugged at the slicker till it came loose. From the officer's waist he pulled something long and thin and pointed it at the sky. With his dirty thumb he pressed a button on the hilt and sparks glittered up the double prong of the power-blade.

Nail-bitten fingers, like sprung clamps, released bruised necks as the beefy man's face twisted in the light. His lips rolled back from a broken tooth and the corners of his eyes crinkled like paper.

The young woman ceased her moan, and even the old woman paused, groping to straighten the tin circle which dimmed and brightened in the blade's wavering light. "That," she said after a whispering exhalation, "certainly isn't it. But never mind. Bring it along, anyway. Somebody stole it from me, I'm sure. But we'll find it, don't worry. Come along, there! Don't dawdle! Come along now!"

As the boy raised his head the hair fell back from his eyes. Reflected sparks shot from tear to tear on his cheek.

"Through here," Jon said, motioning her towards the alley.

"What about the broken water main?" asked Alter.

"It can't be that deep. Just wet. They've blocked off almost every other way to the wharf. We'd just have to go around to the airfield to get through."

"We both know how to swim," Alter shrugged.

"Come on." Down the block Jon could see lights gleaming on the flooded street. They looked like sheets of black glass.

"Ever notice how dark alleys make you whisper?" She glanced at the warehouses, and the windows of empty stores drifted past. Their feet began to slap water.

As they passed under the light the inverted face of a

building, its dusty windows, the black wound of the doorway and lopsided steps, shattered under their sandals. Their footsteps lisped as they slogged forward. The back of his hand occasionally brushed her wrist; her shoulder gently struck his bicep, a physical assurance of mutual presence.

When they reached the corner Jon stopped. With a hand on her shoulder he halted Alter. She blinked, questioning him in the shadows.

His answer was the rising of his chin, the turn of his head denoting gathered attention.

She turned to face the same direction, listening. There was the distant sound of many feet in water.

"Malis?" asked Alter.

"Keep going," Jon said. But when they reached the next corner they stopped again. Something was coming towards them from the cross street.

First, a mark of white fire hovered halfway down the block.

Jon dropped his hand on her shoulder again. In surprise she turned to him. "What is——" Then turned back to see for herself.

The splashing grew, and the white mark became a power-blade, aloft in the hand of a young man in white pyjamas: WARD 739. Behind him, eyes raised to the bright beacon, a dozen figures staggered, shuffled, and reeled.

When what *is* is congruent to what *is supposed* the reaction is functional and the mental processes competent. When what *is* and what *is supposed* have nothing to do with each other the choice of reactions is random. Something tears. Stay or run, laugh or frown: the decision is chance. Malis are supposed to lurk, vicious and malevolent, in the night streets of the city. But these were like no malis they had ever seen. Jon and Alter stayed and frowned.

So when the tall woman suddenly pointed a furious, quivering finger, crying, "Of course! They must have it! Quick! Catch them before they get away!" Alter and Jon were off guard. The hesitant half-movements of the figures found focus: someone dived at Jon's legs and pulled them from under him so that he fell. Someone else yanked Alter by the arm, and three hands caught her shoulders.

As their minds worked to pull shredding reality together she cried, "Jon, look! That woman!" She tried to ignore the fingers holding her, but her hands were still free below the elbow. Her left hand grabbed at her right elbow joint, holding to it as if it were in pain—or pain remembered.

Jon said, "My lord, that's the Queen Mother. That's King Let's mother!"

"But she's supposed to be in the psycho ward of——"

"—of the General Medi——" Midway through Jon's word, realization of who these people must be, struck Alter. And a fist of nail-bitten fingers struck the side of Jon's head so hard that he slumped unconscious into the arms of the girl with runny eyes who had begun to coo.

The woman in the tin crown rushed towards Jon, then stopped, her sheet swaying from her extended arms. "He must have it! He has stolen it!" She squatted before Jon. "All right, what did you do with it! Where did you take it! Answer me, I say! Don't you know whom I am?" She jumped up and seized the power-blade from the youth——

"Your Majesty!" Alter cried, her words broke terrified through the recalled agony of her arm. "Your Majesty, please——" She was still holding her elbow, and the words were a frightened, raucous whisper.

The blade stayed in the air. The old head turned, damp

hair stringing her cheeks. "You . . . you called me Your Majesty," the old woman said in the queer voice. "You called me Your Majesty? Do you really know who I am?"

"You are . . . the Queen Mother, mother of the King, Your Majesty. Don't hurt him."

The sword fell to her side. She straightened herself. "Yes," she mused. "Yes. That's right. But he has—has stolen it from me, I'm sure." Her eyes focused on Alter again. "I am the Queen. Yes. But none of them believe me." She motioned to the people about her. "I have told them all, again and again. But *they* don't think I'm really the Queen. Oh, they follow me, because I say so. Sometimes they do what I say, because I get angry when they disobey. But—but they don't . . . don't really believe me." She removed the circle of tin from her head. "See, they took my crown. I had to make this tin one for the one they took away. How will anyone know I am really the Queen with a tin crown?"

Alter closed her mouth, opened it again, then said: "I know it, Your Majesty. As for your crown, it is the idea, not the object that is important."

A smile broke in the old woman's face. "Yes. That's right. You do know who I am?" She set the crown back on her head, then reached towards Alter's neck. Alter cringed into the arms of the man and two women who held her. But the finger lifted the leather necklace with its shells. "This is a beautiful piece of jewellery," said the woman. "I almost seem to . . . to remember it. Do I have one like it myself? Perhaps I . . . accidentally broke one like it, a long time ago?"

"Perhaps," whispered Alter.

"You must be a countess. Or a princess of the royal family to wear such jewellery."

"No, Your Majesty."

"But it is of the sea. At least a Duchess or——But one gentlewoman never inquires after the rank of another. I am forgetting myself." She let the necklace fall. "To know you are of my family is enough." She turned again to Jon. "But him! He has stolen it, I know. I will kill him if he does not give it back to me!"

"Your Majesty," cried Alter, "he is my friend, as noble a man as I am a woman."

"He is?"

"Oh, yes, Your Majesty. He's taken nothing from you."

"You're sure?"

"I'm very sure."

"Then where could it have got to? Someone must have it!"

"What . . .what are you looking for?" ventured Alter.

"I can't . . . oh, I can't remember," wailed the Queen.

"But you must—keep looking. It isn't here," Alter whispered.

Immediately the old woman began to search through the creased sheet that served her for a robe. "I know I had it just a while ago. They took my crown, my sceptre, even took away my—— Oh, I can't find it anywhere. . . ."

"Even taken away your pockets," Alter said softly, tilting her head in sudden wonder.

"Even my pockets," repeated the Queen, still picking over the sheet. "Everything aristocratic is gone. They have taken it away. No one believes me. I must wear a silly tin crown. It's all gone. They've taken——" Then a tendon in her neck quivered beneath the folded skin. Her eyes moistened. She raised the flashing blade and turned to Jon. "He stole it! I know he did! If he doesn't give it back I'll——"

The hands that held her had loosened, and Alter suddenly lunged forwards and wrested Jon from the grip of the cooing girl. On her knees she turned to face the sword. "Won't you do one decent thing in your life? Leave him alone!" The blade halted, and in the silence, Alter heard the quick splashing of feet as someone fled down the street, someone else who must have wandered upon the scene, observed from just around the corner, at last to flee terrified at this point, some mali this time who would have fought with fists and weapons, but even himself is defeated by this insanity. "Your Majesty," she said again, pushing the other thought away, "don't hurt this man. You are the Queen. I should not have to tell you how . . . how little it behooves the Queen to show such anger when no offence was given. If you are the Queen be merciful."

"I—I am the Queen?" The inflection suddenly rose to interrogative in the middle of the last word. It kept rising into a wail. Tears squeezed between the wrinkled tissue of her lids. "I remember," she cried. The blade dropped in the water and shorted out in a hiss of steam. "I remember now. It was the picture." She backed away. "The picture of my son."

Slowly she turned away, her voice still coming aimlessly back to them. "I had two sons, you know." As she walked off the others began to follow her. "They stole my youngest from me, then they murdered my eldest. But I had a picture, a miniature picture with a metal frame, about the size of my palm, a picture of my son. It was the kind vendors used to sell for half a unit down by the wharves. But they stole it from me. They wouldn't even let me keep that. Everything, everything is gone. . . ."

Now the hemp-haired brute lumbered behind her chuckling. Almost in slow motion the boy from WARD 739 picked up the shorted blade and raised the dull prong into the air. Once more the girl began her cooing and followed them down the street. After them the others disappeared into the alley, each unsteady footstep shattering their inverted images on the reflecting water.

Jon was moving. As he sat up, Alter pressed her face against his damp shirt, her breath coming in staccato gasps. "Jon—You didn't see—you didn't see her . . ."

His arm locked around her shoulder. "I wasn't that far gone," he said. "I heard the last couple of minutes."

"Talking to her," Alter said, at last capturing the breath that fled her lungs and would not stay, "without screaming was the hardest thing I've ever done."

Jon pushed himself to his feet. "Well I'm glad you did it. Let's get to that damn boat, and hurry. Hey, relax," he added. "You can let go of your arm now. You're safe."

Alter took another deep breath and looked down where her left hand had again fastened around her right elbow. "I guess I can, now," she said, and after a moment dropped her hand to her side.

They reached the cobbled waterfront as the moon cleared the sea, scattering flaked silver. They made their way to the docks of the tetron tramps.

They came on board, registered, and minutes later the dirty boat lugged away from the docks into the flickering swell. They leaned on the rail, looking at the hollow shadows of each other's eyes, then to the diminishing spires of the city, then back to the shaking, moonlit sea.

"How many times have you made this trip to the mainland?" Jon asked.

"A couple of times with the circus when it was on tour," she said. "Then that spurt back and forth through the transit-ribbon right at the beginning of this whole business. But that's all." She waited while the smile she could feel him smiling but could not see became sound and floated away under the noise of the wash on the hull.

"For me," Jon said, "there was the time I was carried off to the penal mines, and then when I got out I got back via the transit-ribbon. There was the time we first took Let to the forest. And, three years later when we brought him back." He turned to her, to the shadows that were her eyes, her white hair moon silvered, blown from the curve within curve of her ear. "Now we're here." A wave larger than the others threw spray at their faces. "Alone together."

"What's being alone, or being with somebody?" she asked.

"Or more important," he said, feeling somehow he was speaking her thought more precisely, "why do you feel alone, even when you're with somebody one time —and at others . . . well, not alone."

The drop of her head, the release of a muscle in her cheek shifting the moon-shadow there told him it was her thought.

"When I know the answer to that one . . ." Only he didn't know what he would do, and thought: perhaps what I would do is the answer.

"Remember when we were reading the poems?" she asked. "We were all sort of mixed up in each other."

He nodded.

"What was the poem we couldn't figure out?"

"Another one about loneliness," he said. "I don't remember the beginning."

"I do." She recited, "Equivocal, maniacal, and free as great despair is great tranquillity . . ."

Then a voice behind them continued, and they turned, ". . . Cry in the minions of the ravaged night; turn back, poet, and face the ancient dreams, as tears in moonlight fall by the sea. . . . That's all I can remember."

"Where did you hear that?" Jon asked.

For answer the figure stepped from the shadow of the cabin into the moon. His head was a fuzzy, wrinkled egg, where the nap had been worn from eyes, nose, and mouth, yet thinly covered his chin and scalp. "That's all I remember," he repeated. "How did it end?"

"Solitary people," Jon went on, "by the sound of waves trudge the long, soft, sandy ground. Sadness or joy, equal and one, have caused each ended race I have begun."

The sailor sucked his teeth, shook his head, and scratched his stomach with his thumb. "I like that one." His striped singlet was loose over his boney chest.

"Where did you hear it?" Jon asked again.

The old sailor cocked his head, drawling, "And what do you want to know for?" He stopped scratching and pushed a finger at them. "Where did *you* hear it?"

"We read it," Alter said. "Please tell us, won't you?"

He shrugged and came to the railing. "You make it sound real important." He leaned one hand on the rail. His skinny arm gave and bent as he moved against the rocking of the boat. "Kid with that funny couple told it to me. He said he wrote it."

"A kid, with a couple?"

"He was maybe twenty-one, twenty-two. To me that's a kid. All three of them were going across. Kept to their rooms most of the trip. The guy wore this funny hood. But the kid was all over the place, talking with everybody, reciting these poems he'd written. That was one of the ones he told me."

"Catham would be wearing a hood to cover that plastic face of his if he had to leave quickly without any viva-foam," Jon said.

"No wonder there were no records of their helicopter leaving for the mainland. They must have ditched it back in the city and taken the boat over." She stopped. "Jon, he said Nonik was running around, talking to everyone, excited, happy. That doesn't sound like anyone whose wife was just——"

"I didn't say happy," interrupted the sailor. "That's your word. More sort of hysterical. He'd ask people strange questions, and then wait for an answer like a puppy whose paw you just stepped on. But sometimes he'd get up and walk away three-quarters through what you were saying."

"That sounds more like it," Jon said. "How long ago was this?"

"Same day the military ministry got bombed in Toron."

"So they went to the mainland too," said Jon. "Where did they get off?"

"Boat only makes one stop on the coast. They got off right where you'll be in a couple of hours."

They pulled up nearly an hour before sunrise. The boat would receive its cargo at noon, when most of the passengers would disembark. "Sure you don't want to wait till daylight?" asked the sailor. He was sitting on an overturned bucket, carving a mop handle into a series of leering totems. "Lots of malis around here, and nighttime is mali time." He held the pole braced in his toes and picked carefully at distorted smiles and gaping frowns, the short knife blade *tic-tac-ticcing*.

"We want to get a good start," said Jon.

The moon was large and low on the horizon, and when

97

the sailor nodded to them the thin shadow of the mop handle swung across the deck.

"What is that?" Alter asked, pointing to a shadowy hulk down the docks.

The sailor looked up. "The circus ship."

"But what's wrong with it?" It was tilted sideways, and even in the moonlight one section of the red-and-gold hull showed black blisters over half its length.

"What does it look like," the sailor said. "I told you there were malis around. That happened maybe a month ago."

"What happened?" Jon asked.

"When the circus came back to tour the mainland malis attacked, fired the ship, broke up the place. Killed a lot of people——"

"——killed?" asked Alter.

The sailor nodded.

"Oh, Jon!" She looked back to the wreck. "I was working for them——"

"Come," he said. At his touch she began to walk down the sloping ramp, turning her white head now and again to look at the ruined ship.

Walking up the boardwalk, Jon asked, "Do you think Clea, Catham, and Nonik might be somewhere around here?"

"Why?"

"Clea also used to work for the circus. Maybe she came back to get something she'd left." Across a field in the horizontal moon, tents still flapped on their guys. "They probably won't be here now, but maybe they passed through."

"I can show you which was her tent," said Alter. They turned to the meadow. Breezes sped to the sea and bent the grass towards the waves, as beyond the sand the crushed ivory foam broke and spumed to the meadow. They neared a rippling wall of canvas. As they stepped towards the entrance a figure moved:

"What do you want out here?" His trousers were from a soldier's uniform, but the sleeveless vest that laced over his chest was fisherman's apparel. His blond hair was a short brush of military cut three months gone.

"We're just looking through the tents," Jon said.

"Who said you could look?"

"Who said we had to ask?"

"We don't like strangers too much, snoopin'. There been all sorts of mali stuff about. The town"—he motioned with his chin towards the collection of houses across the meadow—"don't want no strangers around. Malis raided them last week. Killed a couple of people. Didn't steal nothing. Just broke up the place." He let out a short laugh. "Isn't that something?"

Jon frowned as the tent wall rippled faster, then stilled. "Hey, what's out there?" came a voice from behind the canvas.

Lyn called back over his shoulder, "I don't know, Raye."

A second figure stepped to the first one's side. "You think they're malis?" Raye, younger, darker, also wore a disorderly soldier's uniform.

"Could be," Lyn shrugged.

"We're not malis," Alter declared. "Did the town station you out here to keep malis from moving into the tents?"

"Could be," Lyn shrugged, then laughed again. It was a quiet, windy sound: the voice of a man who had lived by the sea's edge, with something in it of water over rock.

Raye laughed too. Laughter was coming from behind them as well.

They turned and the laughter rose. Nearly twenty more were standing behind them. Now they closed ranks, circling. Many wore remnants of army uniforms; most were green-eyed and dark. Two were girls. The laughter broke in peak after liquid peak. "They say they're not malis," Lyn said again. Like a wave rolling back across sand, the sound ceased.

Jon was afraid. He was also thinking fast.

"Bet you can't prove it," someone called.

"You know what we do to . . . malis."

"Come on, let's show them what we do to malis!"

Seconds later, he and Alter, their arms held tight behind them, were marched through the tents. One man had gratuitously socked Jon's jaw, and it throbbed. But he was thinking, meticulously and quickly. The man guiding him once jerked him as they passed several mounds of earth.

"That's what *you* townies do to *us* malis," Raye hissed, then pushed them violently past the graves.

"What makes you think we're from town," Jon got out.

"I don't care where you're from."

Jon heard Alter draw a quick breath at some injury he could not see, since she was behind him.

A fallen carpet of yellow canvas spread over the grass in the ivory stain of moonlight. They were approaching the line of aquarium wagons, locked end to end. There was talk behind him that Jon tried to correlate:

"Which one do you think'll try to save the other? Which one do you think'll run?"

"I say flip: heads we tie him up and let the girl try to save him, tails we tie the girl and see what he does."

"Don't leave it to chance. I want to see a good show. Tie up the girl and throw him in with the knife."

"Hell, he'll run. How much you want to bet he's a coward and runs."

"Tie him up, and the girl is sure to bolt."

"We'll still have some fun. She won't get very far."

Now Lyn's more forceful voice settled it. "Put your money away. We tie her and give him the knife. He won't let them at her without putting on some sort of show."

Alter was pushed on to the canvas. Someone brought a rope and her arms were bound. Once they exchanged glances, neither imploring nor despairing, but rather looks of desperate concentration as each tried to find the flaw in the net of action and movement carrying them to unnamed doom. Now Jon was pushed forward on the collapsed tent.

They were shoved towards the row of aquariums. Moonlight through the misted water caught sailing shadows that darkened window after window. The water was green with algae. The tanks had not been cleaned for a long time. The great octopus that had been exhibited there had probably been the first to die from the impurities. The dolphins must have gone next, poisoned by the unfiltered water. The manta ray, a scavenger by nature, might well have survived the longest in the foul drink, but at last it, too, must have succumbed and floated belly upward on the scummy surface. The only large creatures left were the sharks. Great and gaunt, they would be the last to die of filth. Now they swam lazily back and forth nosing the glass and the corners of the tanks.

A platform with a wooden ladder had been built by one wagon's edge. Jon and Alter were man-handled to its foot, and then up on the platform at the tank's rim. What happened next—it happened inside Jon's mind—was a marshalling of dispersed bits of information, of learning and fragments of learning, of conjecture, action, and random chance. He was still afraid, but suddenly there was a bright line leading across the glistening sands of panic.

The tanks had once been separated by a system of locks so that individual tanks could be emptied and cleaned. But as the beasts died the six-foot walls between the wagons had been removed, and more water had been let in till the tank was full to the brim once more. Opened and connected, they formed a single trough twelve feet wide and a hundred and fifty feet long. Green rippled under the moon with the movement of shapes beneath. Each shark —Triton had collected them for size—was a good four hundred, four hundred and fifty pounds. Jon held each fact in his mind as, below him, water lapped the end of the tank.

The sides were raked to prevent anything in the tank from getting out. Raye shoved Alter, still bound, into the water. Jon took a breath and dived as she went off the edge. Water hit him of indifferent temperature. He curled up, sinking from momentum, and tore off one sandal. The pressure on his ears was lessening, which meant he was rising towards the surface again. He tore off the other sandal, broke surface, and threw his head back, to shake the water from his face. He took a last look at what was happening on the surface: to balance and separate the relevant from the irrelevant. Alter near the end of the tank was bobbing rhythmically. With a controlled scissor kick, a good swimmer can tread water a fair amount of time, even with hands tied: Alter was a good swimmer (relevant).

"Hey there!" one of the malis called from the

platform—it was a girl (irrelevant)—she jammed something into the air, a knife (relevant), then flung it into the water. He dived for it, following its glittering spiral to the depths of the tank as a shadow passed over him, thinking, Should I cut the ropes that bind Alter's hands so—— The thought became an irrelevancy as he grabbed the blade from the gravel flooring: the edge of his hand nicked! The knife was so sharp that with himself moving and Alter moving, there would be no way to avoid a few cuts and scratches. Blood in the water meant death.

Was that how the others thrown bound and free here had perished (irrelevant)? He started swimming underwater, and broke surface forty feet down the tank, took another breath and drove forward again. How long would it take for the beasts to become curious. Seconds, minutes? The farther apart he and Altar were, the greater the sharks' indecision. He put the blade between his teeth to free his hands for swimming. Moving beneath the surface attracted less attention than splashing over the top. He shot forward, through water like rutilant glass.

A shark nosed so close his glaucous flesh gleamed. To the surface for three breaths; he dived again, muscles electric and alert, and silently thanked Alter for her patient training (pushing down the thought of banked teeth raking those muscles; and Alter was bound).

Another dive brought him to the far end of the aquarium (which of the beasts had turned and turned in the central flood, deciding between the two figures, and chosen her, legs scissoring in free fog, white hair awash about her face). He grabbed the knife from his teeth and would have used his own flesh, his own blood to bait his plan; but something moved at the edge of his blurred, submarine vision, and he whirled and plunged the blade into it, catching it against the glass. It was a fair-sized fish, over a foot long, but grown sluggish in the diseased water. Now it flipped and squirmed in veils of blood. Jon seized the fish and ripped the knife upward towards the blood-rich gills and pressed the bleeding carcase against the glass. He reversed himself in the water (remembering her words, "Put your head back. Now bring your knees up and roll backwards," realizing this was the same motion) and swiped the bloody meat down the side of the glass, leaving a dissolving track of red.

One instant he felt himself in blind subjection to all the factors he could not control, all that was desperate and jagged in both inner and outer environment; as he perceived it, it turned over in his mind, like a spinning coin dropping with him through the water. The other side was a sense of total control that came with the extent of his perception. He shot to the bottom of the tank, leaving a column of blood. The coin spun.

Sound travels faster in water than in air. He heard them coming, flung the fish away, then jammed himself from the glass wall, pushing with his feet. His palms scraped over the gravel and the water darkened with thunderous shapes.

Crash!

He rolled over, away from the pain in his scarred hands.

Crash! Crash!

Two more struck the wall separately. Then—

—*Cruuuummm!*

—two struck at once, and tide jerked him upwards. His head jammed through the surface at the same time he heard the three-inch glass plates crack. He was flung into foaming air. It had worked!

With the locks removed and the extra water the pressure

in the aquariums was almost five times what it was intended to be, and well over what theoretically it could be. Some chance structuring had kept the walls together. But a few blows from a couple of four-hundred-and-fifty-pound, hungry sharks barrelling down a hundred-and-fifty-foot run had done it.

He struck the ground on wet grass. Remembering his falls, he flipped over and sprung open to a standing position. He staggered in the streaming weeds, panting for the agonizing breath he had held. The knife was still in his hand. Droplets became pearls as they ran down the blade in the gibbous moon.

Three of the grounded sharks twisted and flopped on the grass. He turned to the shattered wall of the aquarium. Raye, for whatever random reason, had run to this end of the tanks to watch. When the wall exploded he had been nearly severed by a shard of glass that gleamed in his ruined belly.

Jon ran to the wagon, vaulted up the waterfall, and splashed down the gravel flooring of the tanks. Alter lay face down twenty feet from the end, washed there before the level became too low to carry her farther. It couldn't have been more than thirty seconds since the wall first broke! But he was aware how accelerated his time sense was. Even so, she couldn't have—— He was already beside her. He pulled her from the water.

Alter opened her eyes and her mouth at the same time and sucked in air. Then her eyes closed again, but she kept on gasping. Jon sawed the ropes from her arms. He scratched her a couple of times, but the ropes fell away, and she hunched her shoulders and spread her elbows (and he remembered the exercise she had taught him to get the blood back into your arms) and staggered to her feet.

He pulled her to the jagged rim, jumped out, and helped her down.

Malis were running along the side of the wagons: recovered from their shock at the explosion (an aquarium is not *supposed* to explode; but it *did*—the paralysis had lasted nearly three-quarters of a minute), they were coming to recover their prey.

Jon and Alter ran through the wet meadow, strewn with glass, avoiding the long, frantic shapes flopping about them.

Alter was exhausted. Jon felt it as her wrist shivered in his hand. He himself was moving on energy left in the glowing ends of burned-out nerves. Their running became a fast walk. When they were halfway to the forest someone screamed behind them; panting, they turned to look.

One of the malis had passed too close to a shark. The animal had flipped and caught her by the leg. The others were trying to help. Jon filled his raw lungs with one more breath, and stumbled forward. He kept stumbling until leaves were striking him in the face, and the screaming had stopped.

They reached a clearing five minutes into the wood where the rocks sloped up for twenty feet. Halfway across the granite rise, Jon turned.

A quarter of the sky had gone grey with dawn. Each tree about him cast a double shadow with the glow of the old moon and the new rouge of the sun. Alter sank to the rock and ran her hands back over her forehead, smoothing her wet white hair into a helmet. Suddenly she hunched over, as if to hold what little strength was left in the cave of her body.

At the same time Jon felt the emergency catches that had tautened his body into a survival machine start to release, one after the other: his shoulders, the backs of his hips, his calves; his bruised palms began to sting. He lowered himself beside her, each muscle like a metal weight dropping into the acid of fatigue. She raised her head and said, softly and wonderingly, "We're safe!"

Jon pressed his head against her shoulder, as she had done at a similar moment in the city, relaxing in the reality of wet skin against wet skin. She put her hand on the back of his neck, and after a moment he raised his head and looked at her.

The breeze hesitated in the branches, quivering among the leaves before it rolled on.

"I can see your eyes," Jon whispered. "There's enough light now so that I can see your eyes."

CHAPTER EIGHT

EACH person moves towards whatever maturity he is seeking in a definite direction. He approaches each observed incident from that direction, sees it from that one side; but it may not be the same side someone else sees. In Toron, when Alter cried to the Queen, "Won't you do one decent thing in your life!" a young mali who had come upon them before, at that point, turned and splashed off through the night. It was Kino.

We cannot trace here the experiences that brought the gutter youth to the point where this sentence, out of the whole exchange, struck him, tripped something in his mind that brought him up short, stayed with him when the rest of the incident had joined the many inexplicable things he had seen on the streets. He did not recognize Jon. He made no connection between the maundering speech and the hospital clothing. But for his own reasons, this hysterical imperative was what he contemplated as he fled from the blocked-off section, slipped past the guards, and came to the waterfront.

Pondering, he took a piece of chalk from his pocket and wrote over a peeling war poster: *You Are Trapped in That—*

"Kino?"

"Jeof?"

Kino turned.

"You the one writing that stuff all over the walls?"

"Some of it," Kino said, frowning into the shadows. The neo-neanderthal emerged into the livid moonglow. On the wharf cobbles a breeze tugged at a piece of paper stuck there by the damp.

Kino wondered if he should stay or go. "What are you doin' out here, Jeof?" he asked to avoid the decision.

"My territory," Jeof grunted. "You gonna say I can't walk around in it?"

"No, Jeof. I didn't mean nothin' like that."

"Fall out, Kino," Jeof said. "I'm in deep water."

"I'm going," Kino said. He put the chalk in his pocket. Then he stopped. "Jeof, have you ever done one decent thing in your . . . well, done something you could be proud of?"

"I'm proud," Jeof said, his voice lowering. Both hands rose, open palmed, then snapped to fists in the foggy light. "I'm proud."

Kino drew back, but went on: "Proud of what, Jeof?"

"You better fall out."

"In a minute, in a minute. No, really Jeof, what the hell

are you proud of?'' Features readjusted themselves on the neanderthal face: brows flattened, cheeks sunk, the bar of muscle at the back of his jaw contracted. ''Nobody else is proud of you. After that business with Nonik's wife, you think fish around here think you're big? Naw. You're a very small ape. And maybe you're so small, they think you shouldn't even be around. Maybe there's a group of them right now sitting down somewhere trying to figure out how they can get you and tear you in little pieces, like you did her. And maybe they're gonna start looking for you at about ten o'clock tonight. And maybe they'll be coming over from the inn, where they're planning it now, to hunt you out of your little hole in the ground so they can stomp on you, ape.'' The last paragraph was total fabrication. Kino, having started talking, had seen the chance to revenge his friend.

''Why are you telling me, then?''

Kino shrugged. ''I just like to warn people. I do it all the time.'' He felt his ability to keep up the bluff begin to fail. ''See you around—I hope,'' he added, and turned away. The same fear that had caused him to fabricate the vendetta had crushed the delicate concern for Alter's sentence. Now he hurried down the street thinking, Well, I scared him some! Bet he walks around a little more carefully now!

We cannot trace the experiences that bring a man to observe a given phenomenon from a given side. Relative to our limited perception, much of his reaction is random.

Jeof stood alone on the cobbles. The paper, stuck to the ground, ripped in the breeze and flapped up the alley. Once more he clenched his fists and let Kino's words pick their way through his mind. ''I'm proud,'' he mumbled, and then, ''At least I'm proud.'' He looked up, and suddenly his frown twisted all out of shape into an expression with no name. "They'll never find me," he whispered, and lurched forward.

What routes rage followed in his brain, what directions and misdirections it took, what caused him to judge and misjudge, also we cannot trace here.

Two blocks later he stopped, panting, in front of a small door at the bottom of three stone steps. He dropped down all three and landed with his fist pounding.

There were several secret shops in the Devil's Pot where thieves could pick up illegal power-blades heisted from a guard transport; stolen government explosives; much of the intricate equipment, made for an unfought war, had gone astray as it moved from storehouse to storehouse. These shops disappeared often and did much of their business at night. When the door was opened a crack Jeof pushed inside.

Five minutes later he took all three steps in one motion and started back down the street. In one stubby hand he held a brass sphere with a stud on one end. It was a small, powerful grenade. He had once lobbed its twin through the window of a crematorium whose manager hadn't wanted to pay protection. The burst of flame and glass, the brightness and glory, hung in his mind divorced from the destruction, a protected instant of light.

At the cellar mouth he halted. They would look first for him there. The alleys where he often slept on lean evenings were not safe. Other malis were constantly poking around in them, and he would be found out. He turned up the waterfront street where the mercury-lights hung in shields of fog.

A gate to one of the piers had been left open by accident. He crossed the street and went through. There was only one boat at the dock. Jeof hesitated. At the gangplank the chain had also been left off. The small inter-island launch was dingy and unpainted. Its captain had been careless, gone off without closing up anything. Probably nothing worth stealing on it anyway, thought Jeof as he climbed on to the deck.

The boat rose and settled in the sludge that licked the city. Jeof rubbed the grenade against his hip. Another night he might have broken the windows, or found a bucket of paint and messed up the deck; tonight he was just going to hide.

As he reached the hatch a whining sound overhead made him look up. Then, beyond the buildings of the wharf, he saw a distant explosion. Jeof sucked disgustedly at his lower lip and started down into the musty hole. Another freak bombing. Keep on and blow up the whole damn city, he thought, between statement, question, and speculation. Maybe it would distract the pack hunting him—give them something to go loot. He sat in the damp corner and put the grenade in his lap. Let them come after him here. He wondered where the explosion was. The boat's movement made the darkness about him shift and sag like a half-jelled solid.

Let ran forward into the billowing smoke. It rasped the rims of his nostrils, abraded the back of his throat. He screamed, "Petra, where are you?"

Light flared to his right from an opening door. Coughing, someone stumbled into him. "Let, what in the world—?"

"We've been bombed, Petra. *We've* been bombed!"

Wind nudged the smoke from between their startled faces. As she stared about, Petra cried out, jerking the back of her hand over her mouth. Part of the ceiling and far wall had torn away. As a light connection broke and the last light in the hall went out, they saw the glittering bubble of the night.

She seized him by the shoulder and fled down the hall as behind them the roar of falling stone swelled, then faded to chuckling shards. "This way." She started up the left-hand stairwell.

"Petra!" He caught her back. "We'll have to go the other way." A slab of plaster had fallen from the wall, and beyond that were piles of brick. They turned back over the fallen struts and up the other stairway.

It was only after they passed the palace guard, crumpled on the steps with his head under a block of masonry, that fear realized itself, as in a mirror where the drape has been ripped away.

"Where were we hit, Petra? Are they still bombing?"

For answer thunder filled the hall and they felt the floor shake. Glass fell before them: the crystal of the ceiling chronometer had broken.

In another room down another hallway someone screamed.

"What about the council wing?" Let asked as they started down the next stairwell.

"I think that's where the first bomb struck," she said.

"Otherwise, we'd be dead. Come this way." They turned through a door that let them out on the upper balcony of the throne room.

As they rushed past the columned railing, Let cried out, "Petra!" He pointed down into the hall. Only one of the lights burned at the end of the room. People moved over the floor below, fingers of shadow jutting from each. "Petra, look!"

She joined him at the railing.

"What are they doing, Petra? Who are they?"

She put her hand on his shoulder, and he felt her press down.

"What is . . . ?" he began. Then, in response, he crouched. The Duchess stooped beside him.

"So soon . . . " she whispered, shaking her head. "So soon . . . They're here already—"

"What *are* they?"

"Look."

The figures moved below, glancing right and left in wonder. Now one ran to the window, grabbed a drape, and tugged till it ballooned down over him. The others laughed, but the first one wrapped the brocade hanging about his waist and trailed it behind him back to the others. Another man, stopping before the jewelled inlay on the wall, was industriously prying at the glitter with the point of a knife. A third hastily shoved something under his tunic, snatched from a pedestal which had held some historical statuette.

"Looters, marauders, vandals," whispered Petra, "—malis."

Suddenly three new figures burst into the throne room from the far entrance: two elderly men and a woman. Their dress was as rich as the vandals' was poor, but torn, dusty, and charred as well.

"They're from the council," Let whispered. "They must have just escaped from the council wing."

The three and the many faced each other over an electric moment. Then the man in the brocade drape stepped foward. "What you doing here?" he demanded.

The councilmen, numbed by their escape, only moved closer to one another.

The speaker, emboldened by their silence, cried again, "What are you trying to do to us here?" A rush of guilt came with his next words. "You have no business here. You can't keep from the . . . the people what is rightfully theirs!"

In bewilderment, rather than negation, the council members shook their heads. Councilwoman Tilla's hand went nervously to the collar of sea agates at her throat. Councilman Rillum fingered the end of his gold belt. "We were only trying to get away from—" began Councilman Servin, collecting himself.

But a vandal cried out, "Don't let them get away! They'll tell! They'll tell! Don't let them go!" And suddenly they surged at the cowering trio.

Then one man was waving the sea-agate collar in the air, and a woman ran towards the door trailing the gold belt behind her.

Petra's grip tightened until the King winced. Realizing how tight she held him, she dropped her hand. "Let . . ." she whispered. "Oh, my King . . ."

"Petra?"

"Like this? Oh, not like this!"

"Petra, perhaps what you said about the aristocracy is right. Maybe it's better that it go—"

She turned to him abruptly, eyes raging in the long shadows from the single light. "The aristocracy," she repeated. "At its worst, a sargasso of every conceivable neurosis society may have; by naming itself it has agreed to its own death. But at least it has had the dignity to applaud its own order of execution in the past if the document is eloquent." She turned back to the railing and gazed down at the floor, empty save for three twisted

114

bodies at the throne's foot. "But this . . . No, not like this . . ." Again she shook her head. "Even in the people, now, all that is aristocratic is gone."

"In the forest," Let said after a moment, "they would say, all that is histosentient is gone."

The Duchess looked at him questioningly.

"All that is human is gone," he translated.

Footsteps behind them. Then: "There they are! There! That one must be the King!"

They ran without looking, down the balcony, and turned into the maze of hallways.

"We'll catch them! It's just a woman, and the kid's got a limp!"

But they were not caught. They knew the palace labyrinth where the looters did not. At last they stood deep in an alcove of the little park behind the castle. "Now you follow me!" the King whispered suddenly.

"But where—"

The boy started forward, however, and she followed. Through one door, over a little bridge and under an arch; they were hurrying by the wall that ran along the Avenue of the Oysture. When they reached the hive-houses she asked again, "My King, where are we going?" She looked back where the flames tongued between the spires of the city.

"Come!" Now it was he who held tightly to her shoulder. "There's nothing we can do now, Petra. Come with me, please!" In a moment she turned and came.

The city was in panic. People rushed from their homes, then rushed back in to mount their roofs and watch the spectacle. The forces that before had been trying to staunch the broken main were split in half to fight the fires that raged in the city's centre. Random chaos moved and battered through the streets. Making use of the confusion, the two reached the waterfront almost unnoticed.

Silent for the last fifteen minutes, a third time she cried out, "Let, where are you *going*?" She turned again to watch the towers. "Arkor is still somewhere in the castle. Jon and Alter are trying to get to Telphar—"

"And there's nothing you can do," he finished for her. "Please come. Please!"

"But where?"

"To the boats, Petra. We're going to take a boat and go sailing."

"*What*? But, Let . . ."

"Because there's nothing else to do, Petra. And I want to! That's the only reason. If there's nothing that you want to do, at least share this with me."

She was confused, and in her confusion turned to follow him along the piers. Suddenly a group of ragged individuals appeared ahead, and one cried out. "There they are! Look at their clothes!"

They turned and ran along the cobbles. Behind them the cry metamorphosed: "Get their clothes! They must be rich! Get their clothes!"

A quarter of the way down the street a dock gate stood ajar. "In here!" cried the King, and the Duchess followed him. He turned halfway up the gangplank of the single boat and gave her his hand. On the deck she helped him pick up the gangplank and heave it, crashing, to the dock. As they ran to the wheel house, figures filled the gateway.

Petra lingered, staring back. A moment later, something thrilled beneath the deck. The motor's whine set a sympathetic ringing in the chain railing. "Come on up here, Petra! It's moving! We're on our way!"

She turned from the figures crowding the edge of the

pier (and did not see three of them leap from the side of the boat, did not see four hands slip from the deck's edge, nor hear two bodies smack into the froth; nor did she see the two hands that held. Then an elbow cleared the deck, a dark head, another arm). As she joined him at the wheel, her breath was hoarse.

"No, Petra, don't look back at the city. Just keep staring forward! Where shall we go? To your island? To the mainland? Or all the way to the edge of the barrier and beyond? We'll go places no one has ever been, we'll discover new islands all ourselves!"

She looked forward (and did not see the crouching figure start forward, then hesitate at the sound of their voices, glance right and left: the hatch cover was open. On bare feet he darted over the deck that flickered with light from the burning towers and lowered himself into the hole). "Oh, Let, why are—?"

Night flung out over the water, glittering and undulant. "Remember that boy, Petra, who told me about the sun coming up over the sea, burning away the water? Well, for him, then, we'll sail straight into the morning. Whoever he was, we'll sail for him."

"It's night—" she whispered, thinking, *Oh, Let, it's not for him, it's just another selfish gesture, like so many we have made, of the sort that has allowed it all to topple as it has—*

"But soon—" he whispered back, thinking, *Don't you see, Petra, now there is only ourselves to save, there is only this gesture to make, because it has fallen and is no more—*

As each stood on deck, woman and boy, with half-truths straining towards one another to make a whole, below deck Jeof blinked, raised himself to his elbow and felt the motor throb beneath him. Foam hissed outside the bulkhead, and he thought in terror, *Have they come for me?* His stubby hand scooped up the grenade.

A figure descended in the flickering light that fell through the hatch. Jeof pressed himself against the studded plates, the bolts bruising his shoulder. The figure turned, and for one moment his face was fully lit:

"Kino!"

"Jeof!"

He pressed the release, and on the wharf where figures still stared after the craft they saw a momentary blister burn on the water. The brilliance of colliding random energies flung light over their faces, for one moment bright as morning.

CHAPTER NINE

THE breeze rolled back through the forest as they climbed down the dawn-grey slope.

"We'll have to stop in about an hour," Jon said, "to rest."

"Make it a half an hour?"

Jon tried to grin. "Sure."

Something bright and spinning curved through the air and dropped glittering into the leaves before them. "You want to toss that back to me?" someone said from the trees.

They looked from the shadowed leaves to the metal fallen on the ground. Jon bent and picked it up. "Here it is," he said, holding it out. "Come get it."

A hand pushed at a branch and a man stepped forward.

It was difficult to tell his age. Shirtless, ragged pants roped around his middle, the figure walked with one leg slightly stiff. One shoulder was vaguely humped and the right arm dangled limply from its socket. His hairy pectoral shifted as he reached for the coin with his good hand.

Jon pulled it back, though, out of reach. It was a medal with raised figures of several buildings coming to a single peak with a sunburst behind. Along the lower curve, in san serif lettering, was inscribed:

CITY OF A THOUSAND SUNS

Jon frowned and extended it again. Broad strong fingers with wide, dirt-crested nails retrieved it.

"So, you folks want to take a rest? What about clean sheets to rest on, nine inches of mattress to rest the sheets on, and a hydro-spring under that: put the whole thing in a room painted light green where no sound can get through, just morning sun through a window and darker leaves—"

"All right," Jon said. There's a point in exhaustion where such friendly torture can create physical pain, at the back of the throat, the abdomen, behind the knees. "All right, what are you talking about?" Jon repeated.

"Come on, if you want to rest," he said, turned, and started back through the brush.

They fell in behind him more to make questioning easier than to follow: "Where do you want us to go?"

"Didn't you read the signet?"

They climbed boulders, pushed more branches. The morning mist was still thick, and as they pressed at last through dripping foliage, bright light burnished their faces. They were standing on a small cliff that looked down the mountain.

As the golden fog beneath the beating of the sun's

copper hammer fell away, they saw a lake between the mountains. On the lake's edge, people were building a . . . city. The artist who had cut the shape into the medal had idealized it some. On the disc Jon had not been able to tell if the buildings were wood or metal. Most of them were wood. And more structures had been added since the representation had been etched. "What is this place?" asked Alter as they started down the cliff.

"Like it says, they call it the City of a Thousand Suns. They're still building it. It's only been here a little while."

"Who's building it?" asked Jon.

"Malis."

He saw Alter's shoulder stiffen before him as she climbed down.

"Malis," repeated their guide, "malcontents. Only these malis are malcontent with most other malis as well as the rest of this chaotic world." They reached the bottom and stepped on to grass. "So for several years they've been here in the forest, building their city here by the lake."

"Why is it called the City of a Thousand Suns?" Alter asked.

The guide shrugged and chuckled. "Between matter transmission, tetron power, hydroponics, and aquadics, Toromon has enough scientific potential to provide food, housing, rewarding and creative labour for its whole population, and as well to reach out and touch the stars. So a few—a very few people have started to organize such an effort. Anyone who wants is welcome to lend a hand. It's still pretty rough out here, but we can give you a rest. The Thousand Suns are the stars they'll some day reach."

"And us?" Jon asked. "Why did you come out to get us?"

"Well, if you'd kept on the line you were heading you'd have missed it by about four hundred yards. Now if you'd been going straight towards it I wouldn't have had to come and get you. Can't leave everything to chance."

They entered the dusty streets of the town.

Nothing registered very clearly at first. A flush-pump on one corner hawked amber water down a sewage hole. A woman in coveralls was working on it with a small acetylene torch. She pushed her goggles back and smiled at them as they passed. They went by a communications tower where a man on the ground with his hands on his hips was shouting instructions to the man on the antenna. The one in the air wore a military uniform; the tenseness that flattened Jon's stomach was a conditioned response to the dress of the malis he had met earlier. It left when both men turned and waved to Jon's guide.

In one direction Jon saw fields through the wide-spaced houses, and people working in them. In another direction was the lake, and two men, a neanderthal and a forest guard, black against the sun, from opposite ends of an elevated winch, hauled a glittering net from the water.

Order, Jon thought, not as a word, but as the sub-verbal perception with which one might perceive the metre of a fine and devious poem. Alter took his hand. Looking at her wide, staring eyes, he knew she felt it too.

Across the street a cart creaked to a stop before a large building. It was pushed by a forest guard, two men, and a woman. As they stepped back, wiping their wet faces —one man went to the wall fountain and drank from the brass cup below—a group of youngsters came from the building, noisy and laughing. They wore work aprons. The instructor called a young guard, already a head taller than himself, who bent over the motor case at the cart's side. He did something wrong, and the class laughed. The boy looked up and laughed too. He did something right, and the motor began to hum. The instructor spoke appreciately, and then half the class climbed into the cart and it began to roll. Two of the kids, boy and girl, were whistling harmony.

"Come," said their guide, and they turned and continued up the street.

"Who is in charge of this . . . city?" asked Jon.

"You will meet them after you've rested," said their guide. They passed a lawn now where a group of people sat on benches or ambled about.

"These are newcomers," explained the stranger. "You'll be here after you've slept, to talk to our leaders."

A group of children who were obviously not new to the place exploded from one street, laughing and yelling, dashed onto the lawn and dispersed among the adults. Their game had slipped over its peak, for now they broke into smaller, quieter groups.

A young soldier on the bench had taken a handful of coins from his pocket and arranged them beside him in a square with one corner missing. As he flipped a coin into the missing corner, one of the children—a burly neanderthal boy—left his friends and came over to watch, sometimes rubbing his nose. The soldier saw him and smiled. "You want to try?" he asked. "It's a game we used to play in the army, randomax. You see, when I flip this coin into the corner two coins fly off the far side, and we try to guess which ones they'll be."

The boy nodded, "I know that game."

"You want to try a couple of rounds for fun?"

The boy walked to the bench, set the coins in a careful square, then took something from his back pocket. It was a calibrated semicircle with a metal straight-edge that swivelled about its centre. He placed the instrument along the diagonal of the square and sighted the angle. Then he measured the distance, put the free coin there and hunkered down to flip. "Three and five," he said, numbering the coins he guessed would leave. He flipped, and numbers three and five shot from the far edge. He rearranged the square, made another measurement, and said, "Two and five." Flip. Two and five jumped away.

The soldier laughed and scratched his head. "What are you doing with that thing?" he asked as the boy measured again. "You're the first ape I've seen play that well—like a guard almost."

"One and seven," the boy said.

Flip.

One and seven left the far edge.

"I'm just checking the angle of displacement of the line of impact."

"Huh?" asked the soldier.

"Look," the neanderthal youth explained, "the coin you flip has a spin of, say, omega, which in most cases is negligible, so you don't have to worry about the torque. The same goes for the acceleration, as long as it's hard enough to knock at least two coins off and not so hard it'll shatter the entire matrix: call it constant K. The only thing that really matters is the angle of displacement, theta, from the diagonal of the matrix of the line of impact. Once you perceive that accurately, the result is simple vector addition of the force taken through all the possibilities of fifteen—"

"Now wait a minute," said the soldier.

"It shouldn't be called randomax," the boy concluded. "If you perceive all the factors accurately, it isn't random at all."

"That's too deep for me," the soldier said, laughing.

"No, it isn't," the boy responded. "Just think like they teach you in school. Are you going to go to school here too?"

Jon, Alter, and their guide had again stopped to listen. Now Jon stepped to the lawn and touched the boy's shoulder. The soldier looked up, the boy turned; surprise hit their faces, "Who told you that?" Jon asked. "Who showed you how to do that?" It took a moment for Jon to realize that their surprise was at his unshaven, wild appearance, not his question. "Who told you that?" he demanded again.

"The woman," the boy said. "The woman with the man whose head was all funny."

"She had black hair?" Jon asked. "And the man she was with, you could see through half his face, into his head?"

"That's right," the boy said.

Jon looked at Alter.

"Jon," she said, "they're here. . . ."

"Please come with me," said their guide. "You'll have to rest, or you'll collapse."

"They must be here!" Jon repeated, looking about them.

They were taken to a room in a small dormitory building. It was green, and comfortable, and when they woke, it was evening, and the leaves shaking outside their window with the weight of a singing bird were sunset bronze against purple.

"This place," Alter said to the forest guard interviewing them that evening. The window was open, and a warm breeze blew from across the water. "I never thought I would see any place like this in the world I live in. It's something to dream of on another planet."

"It's very much of this world," the guard assured her. "When confusion is great enough the odds are for at least a few people moving in the same direction. Human beings being what they are, order spreads, given half a chance, almost as fast as confusion."

"How do people get here?" asked Jon.

"They hear about it; we have people all over Toromon who come back and forth, a good number of telepathic guards. We need a lot more skilled people, but we're getting them slowly."

"What about my sister, and Catham?" asked Jon. "When can we see them? We have to talk to them immediately. We're coming from Toron. We were sent by the Duchess of Petra, in the name of the King."

"Oh," the guard said, raising his head and putting his hands together.

"We know they're here," said Alter. "We spoke to a little boy who saw them."

"They're not here," said the guard simply. "They were here some time ago. During the days of their stay Clea gave several lectures in advanced mathematics, and taught a few elementary classes. That boy was probably in one. Rolth made quite a helpful evaluation of our economic situation and suggested several ways out of some problems we were already beginning to face. But they were here really only long enough to be married. Then they left."

"Where did they go?"

The guard shook his head. "They said they hoped to return. They also said that they might not."

"Jon, tell him about the enemy. . . ."

"The computer in Telphar?" asked the guard. "We know it has run wild. They may have gone there."

"That's our destination too," Jon said, "if we don't find them."

"Why don't you stay here." There was very little question in his voice.

"We've committed ourselves to finish this," Jon said.

After half a minute's silence the guard said, "Did you know that both the King and the Duchess of Petra, most of the council members, and several other members of the royal family are dead?"

They listened, even after the words had stopped, stunned.

"Toron was bombed again, this time heavily. The royal palace was hit. The city's population is three-quarters destroyed. Evacuees are straggling to the mainland. The report came in late this morning when you were asleep."

Outside they walked to the lake's edge and looked at the ragged mountains. Brass fires extinguished on the water with the ending sunset. The elevated winch dropped a template of shadows on the sand.

"What are you thinking?" she asked.

"About you, and me. That's all that's left, now."

"I'm frightened," she said calmly.

The last sun left the water. "Alter?" he asked, "the boy who gave you your necklace, who died in the war, did you love him?"

She was surprised. "I liked him very much. We were good friends. Why do you ask again?"

Silently he moved through the maze of his thoughts. Finally, he said, "Because I want to marry you. You are my friend. I know you like me. Will you love me too?"

She whispered, and in the variation of her voice he could hear her consider and then answer, "Yes," and softer, "Yes."

He drew her closer and she held his waist. "Marry and stay here," he said. "Alter? If there's nothing left —nothing, then it's wrong . . . And I can't see anything."

"It's what I want to do," she said. "If you hadn't asked me I would have asked you." She paused. "Jon, if there is any meaning to anything—I don't know either. But this one thing we want."

"Then we'll have it."

That night they asked about the city's marriage procedure. They were married the following dawn on a stone platform by the lake's edge as fire mounted on the waves.

CHAPTER TEN

WHILE they were sitting on the lawn with the newcomers waiting to begin orientation, the air was scratched across by the whine of planes. As they looked at the clouds, Jon felt his neck crawl as the sound increased. Alter tensed beside him. Someone else had jumped up. Then the sound faded and they looked nervously back at one another.

The man standing shook his head. "I get stomach cramps every time I hear those damn planes. You wonder where they're going next." He sat back down. "Maybe I should be glad though. I was in the bombing at the penal mines; and if it hadn't been for that I wouldn't be here now. But still——"

"The penal mines?" Jon asked. "The mines were bombed?"

"A couple of days ago," the man explained.

"Why were you in the mines?" Alter asked.

The man chuckled. "From Pot to pit," he said. "It's a pretty hungry story. I was there 'cause I got caught doing whatever I did." He still smiled, though it was clear he didn't want to go into it any more deeply.

"I don't mean to pry," Jon said, "but what's it like now, I mean in the mines?"

"What's it like? If they get any liquor around here some night we'll get drunk together and I'll tell you. But I couldn't take it sober."

Trying to name the urgency within him, Jon said, "You see, I knew someone . . . who was in the mine once, and I . . . wanted to find out what happened to him."

"I see," the man said, more understandingly. "If he was there a couple of days ago"—he shrugged—"the bomb. Who was he?"

"Koshar," Jon said, searching for a name and only coming up with his own. "Did you know Jon Koshar?"

The eyes narrowed, and Jon thought, We squinched our eyes like that, coming from the dark shafts into the purple evenings, the sun blazing on the ferns.

"*You* knew Jon Koshar?" Surprise raised his voice, and Jon waited for him to explain. "The kid who escaped, oh, years ago. You knew him?"

Jon nodded. "What about him?"

"But he *escaped*!" The puzzled smile the man wore asked in itself, Don't you know what that means?

Jon shook his head.

"Let me tell you," the convict said. "I got to prison maybe six months before the Koshar kid escaped. I never knew him, but afterwards guys told me his mess-hall place was just two tables away from mine. But I don't remember him. I knew one of the guys by sight that got killed, the heavy one. But I'd never worked with him or spoken with him. Afterwards, a lot of guys said they had known something was up, but I sure didn't. And I think the guys who said they knew about it all along were just trying to make out like big fish. But I do remember when it happened. My bunk was right by the window, and every night I would go to sleep watching the searchlight glare sweep back and forth outside through the steel net across my window. I woke up once that night just long enough to see it was raining. The net glittered.

"Suddenly officers were shouting outside. A siren started somewhere, and somebody came and banged on the barrack doors with the hilt of his blade. They made first one half of the barracks and then the other come outside and stand in the rain and get yelled at for half an hour. By this time it had gone around that three guys had tried to escape. The guards wouldn't tell us anything, but we knew they must have been pretty successful to cause all the noise. Finally, they let us go back to bed, and with damp hair and bits of grass between my toes, I slipped back under the thin blankets. The next morning when we came out for inspection there were two corpses in the mud.

"As soon as we were dismissed the rumours began; but *three* of them escaped; *one* must still be out! Do you think they got him? What was his name? It was the Koshar kid? Why wasn't he face down in that puddle? Maybe he wasn't in on it and disappeared for some other reason? Naw, I heard from somebody who knew they were gonna make it that he went with them. Then he must still be free. Do you think so?

"Two weeks later there was another attempted escape. They were caught before they started. One of the officers, before he knocked the guy's jaw loose, said, "What the hell did you think you were doing, anyway?" and the guy grinned and said, "I was going out to look for Koshar." That's when it began. Suddenly everybody was talking about Koshar. All sorts of stories sprang up, like how he'd pushed a rock off a guy's foot in a mine cave-in, and one kooky story about him, and another guy who was in for poisoning, messing around a makeshift lab to cook something up for a particularly nasty officer. Almost anything anybody'd ever done there, now they said that Koshar had done it. To stop the talk, they finally told us that they knew he was dead. They said he had wandered out into the radiation barrier and been cooked; that was why his body was never brought back.

"Only the news had the reverse effect. It was as if the fact that the officers thought they could destroy what was important about Koshar by saying he was dead made them laughable. And we laughed at them. That was three years ago. And even when the mines were bombed, three days back, and we were scared to death, the few of us who got out could still laugh a little and say, 'Well, maybe we'll find Koshar after all.'" The man paused. "So you see, when you said you knew him it put me through some changes." He scratched the shoulder of his uniform. "What did you know about Koshar?"

Jon wondered whether his amazement and confused pride showed. "Just that he did escape, even from the radiation barrier."

"He got back to Toron?"

"That's where I . . . met him."

"What was he——" the man stopped, face suspended

in the pleasure of anticipation. Then the smile softened. "—I wonder if I want to know. It would sort of be like the guards saying he was dead. Was he all right?"

Jon nodded.

"Good," the man said. "Maybe some day he'll come to the City of a Thousand Suns and I'll get a chance to meet him myself." He looked around at the buildings. "This is the sort of place he should end up. Does he mean anything special to you? We didn't know him. You did." He sighed, and then laughed. "I have to think about that for a while."

"So do I," Jon said and turned away.

When they had walked to the other side of the lawn. Alter said, "What are you thinking?"

He looked at the grass crushing beneath the toes of his new sandals. "I'm remembering prison; and something I was thinking last night."

"What was it?" she asked.

"Last night I wondered: do I, or anything I've every done, all my attempts to improve myself, the acrobatics and everything, mean anything? When we escaped those characters back at the circus I thought that discipline was the *only* thing that meant something. When we found that the Duchess was dead, and the whole purpose of our coming had exploded, I didn't think anything had meaning—except you. And now . . ." His voice faded.

A neanderthal was coming towards them across the lawn. "Hey there, friends," he greeted them. "I guess I'll be seeing you around here when I get back."

John and Alter looked up.

"First I thought I'd be staying here, but I guess I'm going on." The neanderthal wore a soldier's outfit, and his heavy arms swung in wide arcs.

"You're not staying?" Alter asked. "Why not?"

"Like I explained to the interviewer, I have things to do back with my own people."

"What things?" Alter asked.

The neanderthal reached them, extended his hand, and as she shook it he said, "My name's Lug, what's yours?"

"Alter," she told him. "This is my husband, Jon."

"Glad to meet you both," Lug said. "What I got to do is like this: there's still many of my people not here. I want to teach them things I've learned, things people taught me. Maybe I can even teach them to come back here, huh?" He jabbed at Alter with his elbow and laughed. "Maybe I can teach them to come back here and learn more. But I have to go to them. Besides"—he glanced at the sky—"the dirty planes might even come here. This is all very nice, but it may not be safe either." Again he started and turned to call back, "I see you when I return."

After a moment Alter asked, "Do you want to stay here, Jon?"

"No," he said. "I wanted to marry you, but somehow I got that confused with the quiet and rest and"—he gestured about him—"and this. We've been jerked from one world, to be dropped in this one: but the two are defined by each other, Alter. It can't be safe. I'm going to go on to Telphar, and stop the computer if I can. Do you want to come with me and help?"

She nodded.

"We'll come back too," he told her. "This is a place to come back to when you've finished."

"We'll tell them now," she said.

An hour later they looked back down at the lake.

Someone said, "Don't you want something to remember the place by?" Above them, half hidden by rocks, was the man who had first met them in the woods. With his good hand he tossed the signet towards them. "String it on that necklace of yours, young lady. Look at it sometimes and think of us." By the time Alter picked up the disc, he had disappeared.

Once more they looked back at the City of a Thousand Suns.

"I hope we can come back," she said.

"Then let's go on."

Early in the afternoon from the side of the ravine they spotted ragged, straggling figures groping by the stream. "Who in the world are they?" she asked.

They watched till the group came closer. "More prisoners," Jon said softly.

"I thought maybe malis. *Uh!* they look more like what malis got through with——" She stopped. "Jon, they're women!"

He nodded. "Shafts twenty though twenty-seven were worked by female convicts."

Now they could hear disjointed talk below them. One woman stumbled. The leader took a breath and brushed a grimy hand across her shorn hair. "Come on, baby. We'll never find Koshar like that." She helped the fallen one to her feet.

"We should go down," Alter whispered, "and tell them the way to the City."

Jon stopped her by the shoulder. "The stream they're following goes to the lake. They'll run right into it."

The women moved off into the trees.

After they had started Alter said, "What was it, Jon?"

"I was remembering," he said, "about prison. The men's and women's mines were completely separated, and we never saw anything that even looked like a girl, even though they were only two miles away. It got pretty rough in there, especially for us young guys who had to more or less put up with the older ones if we didn't want to get knocked around a little. The only people who went back and forth were the guards; that's one of the reasons we hated them. There was a standing joke that if there was one thing harder than getting out, it was getting over. Well, probably it was a guard who carried the story, but I guess it got over as well as out."

The trees thinned slowly as they approached the edges of the lava fields. Once a rumbling behind the trees stopped them. They found a vantage point behind a brush-covered rise. Then a tank crashed down the greenery and rolled past. "This must be the final retreat from the 'enemy.' "

"The tanks they had stored there for the 'war' they're using to retreat with now," said Jon.

"How do you think the computer is scaring them off?"

Another tank crashed on behind the first.

"However it is," Jon mused, "it doesn't make it seem like we've got much chance."

The only other thing to give them pause was the group of guards they passed about an hour later. Both the men and women sitting about the clearing bore the triple scars of the telepaths. A breeze shimmered in one black fur cape. One man absently twisted a copper bracelet on his wrist. This was the only movement as the giants engaged in silent communication. He passed through knowing his thoughts were common property to them all. None of them even looked up.

"Were you thinking about Arkor?" he asked when they were minutes away.

"Um-hm."

"Perhaps they know if he's alive, or where he is."

"Another thing to find out when we come back."

At the evening horizon they could see a glow paler than sunset, deadlier than the sea, a luminous gauze behind the hills. They passed the skeletons of ancient trees, leafless, nearly petrified. The crumbly dirt looked as if it had been scattered in loose handfuls, bearing neither shrub nor footprint. By one boulder a trickle of water ran beneath a log, catching light on either side. They looked up.

On the horizon, against the lines of light, as though cut—no, torn from carbon paper, was the silhouette of a city. Tower behind tower rose against the pearly haze. A net of roads wound among the spires.

They could make out the miniscule thread of the transit-ribbon that ran from the city, veering to the right. It passed half a mile away and disappeared over the jungle behind them. Telphar: he felt the word shiver in his brain. "It's so familiar it gives me chills," he said.

"It's pretty creepy looking," she nodded.

They started forward again. A road seeped from under the desert, rising towards Telphar. They mounted and followed it towards the looming city. "It's like going back to some place you've dreamed about before, revisiting some psychotic fanta . . ." He stopped, remembering. Before them the towers were black on rich blue.

"Do you think there's any military left here?" Alter asked.

"We'll find out soon. I'm still wondering how the computer defends itself. Apparently it's got a lot of re-mote-control equipment operating for it, but what does that mean as far as we're——"

Ahead of them, in the shadows, was a rumbling. It

quieted, then grew louder. Suddenly from the gloom of the towers a juggernaut emerged, similar to the tanks they had seen retreating in the jungle, but a superstructure of antennae feathered its roof. A gigantic beetle, it crawled towards them.

"Over the edge of the road," Jon hissed. "You go left, I'll go right."

The tank heaved from the shadow. Across its front in block white letters was stencilled: YOU ARE TRAPPED IN THAT BRIGHT MOMENT WHERE YOU LEARNED YOUR DOOM.

But as they separated, the tank stopped. The antennae ceased whirling and began to swing left and right. The front of the tank rose outward and a man's voice, oddly familiar, called, "Jon, Alter!"

Jon turned to see his wife, half over the opposite road railing, her white hair still swinging from the whirl of her head.

The figure that climbed from the tank was the young man with only one good arm. It was not until he reached the ground that Jon recognized him as their guide to the City of a Thousand Suns.

Behind him, in the tank, were Catham and Clea.

"What are you doing here?" Jon asked, when he had recovered.

"Are you trying to stop the computer?"

Clea shook her head.

Rolth stood in the bubble dome of the tank, looking up at the dark towers about them.

"Then what are you doing?" Jon asked.

From over his shoulder, Rolth said, "We're working."

Jon and Alter looked puzzled, but Clea, instead of answering, turned and walked to Rolth's side. With questioning still in their eyes, they looked to the guide.

"Clea's trying to finish up her unified-field theory, and Rolth is putting the final touches to his historical interpretation of individual action."

"Then why did you come here?"

"For Rolth to finish his theory he had to compare and correlate as many case histories as possible of individual mental patterns. On file in the computer's memory bank are hundreds of thousands of complete psyche-patterns, literally one for every person who had anything to do with the war."

CHAPTER ELEVEN

"And you what are you doing here?" Alter called from across the road.

Jon followed her with a more cogent, "Who are you?" But recognition was already in his voice.

"Nonik," the man said. "Vol Nonik. And you already know these two."

Now Jon recognized his sister. Beside her, the sunset flashed over the plastic inset on Catham's face.

Slowly Jon and Alter moved back together.

"The computer," Jon said, "we came because of the computer. . . ."

"Come in here with us," Rolth said. "We'll take you to the computer."

They exchanged muted greetings as they climbed into the tank. Clea pressed Alter's hand as the door swung to. "I'm so glad to see you." Expectation completed its metamorphosis into achievement. "There's an incalculable amount of atomic and astronomical data that has to be processed and reprocessed before Clea will know whether her theory is correct, and to do it right here is the biggest computer the world's ever known."

"And you?" Alter asked. "Why are you here?"

"The transceivicule!" This from Jon. "The communicators you and Catham have grafted into your throats? What about them, what were they for? They were grafted in right after you left the University."

Nonik laughed softly. "It saved my life, didn't it?" With his good hand he lifted his limp one and then let it flop into his lap. "After they did this to me, after what they did to her . . ." His voice trailed, and both Rolth and Clea turned and looked back at him with worried expressions, but suddenly the voice recovered itself. "Catham was still working on his theory even back then, but he was staying at the University, which meant he was out of touch with a good part of Toromon. It's happened before: you make a beautiful theory about society and psychology; then some guy in the street who doesn't know anything about either comes along and says, 'Hey, you forgot all about such and such,' and there goes your work. I was Catham's guy in the street." He laughed again and called to Catham, "I was to make sure you didn't say anything too stupid in all that abstraction, eh, Rolth?"

"More or less," Rolth called back. "What I wanted was a view of somebody definitely outside society—such as a brilliant mali leader who was an accurate enough observer to be a poet—to check my views against. You helped a lot, Vol."

The poet chuckled again, but once more the sound ended in a middle note, unresolved and tense.

"Did you know Clea at the University?" Alter asked.

"What? Oh. No, only her work," Vol said. "She published a few articles in the math journal, I think it was on the random distribution of prime numbers, wasn't it, Clea?"

"That's right, Vol."

"Fascinating," Nonik said. "Beautiful. Isn't it funny, we can tell exactly what the percentage of prime numbers will be between any two given numbers, yet we still can't arrive at a formula to predict exactly where they are, other than by trial and error. Unpredictable and predictable. The product of the first N primes plus *one* is sometimes another prime. But between the Nth prime and the prime we arrive at there are always others lurking, scattered throughout the real numbers. Like the irregularities in a poem, the quirks in meaning and syntax and imagery that cage the violent, and the very beautiful." Then, whispered and fading, ". . . she was very beautiful . . ."

Again Clea and Rolth looked back. "I guess you could say we knew each other," Clea said. "He'd read my articles, I'd seen some of his poems. He had printed some of them up, and copies of them were being passed around the University. They were very lucid, very clear"—she emphasized the words *clear* and *lucid*, as though they might pull him from his reverie, but he still looked down at the floor—"and put wild and dispersed things into an order that came close to me."

"We're almost there," Rolth said.

One wall of the room was clotted with dials, loudspeakers, tape reels. A few key-punch consoles sat around the floor. "This is one of the control rooms for the computer," Rolth said. "This has been set up for my work. Clea's is down the hall. The machine itself occupies several buildings to the west. You can see them outside that window when the moon comes up. The military has completely abandoned Telphar. We are the only ones left.''

''How does it defend itself?'' Alter asked.

''Quite adequately,'' Rolth said. He went to a small cabinet in the wall, took out a wrench and turned. ''This is purely for demonstration purposes,'' he said, ''do you understand?''

Jon thought he was addressing him, but a voice came from one of the speakers, *''I understand.''*

There were several view screens along the wall, and suddenly Rolth hurled a wrench at the screen's face. The wrench never made it. It stopped in mid-air, glowed first red, then white, then disappeared with a *poof*. ''You see, the computer has managed to take over the whole city, webbed it with induction fields; you are under its constant observation anywhere within its limits. It's self-repairing, and it also has a growth potential wired into its circuits. The thing that they didn't count on was one of the things it managed to learn from all those mind patterns it stored: man has a survival circuit in his brain; I guess that's the best way to describe it. It's a pretty important one, and nobody ever even thought of trying to duplicate it in a machine. But this machine incorporated it into itself while it was 'growing.' It's programmed itself to ignore any programme it's given to cease functioning——''

''About the way you ignore somebody who tells you to drop dead,'' interpolated Vol.

''But when they tried to shut it off by force it began to react accordingly.''

''Suppose the person who told you to drop dead pulled a power-blade on you when you didn't?'' Vol added.

"At first it was just defensive, fouling attempts to dismantle it, occasionally with drastic results. But another thing it had learned from all those warring minds was that if you were offensive once you sometimes save yourself the trouble of being defensive again and again. It quite methodically drove them out. Now it will repel anything it interprets as an offensive action, and after three or four offensive actions from the same source it will try to destroy that source."

"What about you?" Jon asked. "Why are you still here, then?"

"We arrived just before the last of the military was leaving. They were desperate at this point, so they let us have free reign with it."

"But why didn't it reject you with them?"

"This is a very imprecise way of putting it," Clea said, "but it's terribly lonely. We were the only people who were giving it something to 'think' about, something even near its capacity to handle. It's built to work at a certain level for optimum facility, and its survival circuits want it to keep working at that level. Now it's got something to do."

"If it likes you, couldn't you tell it to stop the bombings?"

"It's not that simple," Rolth continued. "All the information it has about Toromon was gathered from the mind patterns of the soldiers while it was manoeuvering them through the war. All of them were wounded by Toromon to neurosis, pushed into pyschosis by the training programme. It hasn't had any need to catalogue and collate all that information, and it reacts on it as a subconscious trauma. It functions as a psychotic."

"Keeping up the analogy," Clea said, "the problems

olth and I are giving it are the closest thing to
sychotherapy it could have. Collating the mental pat-
erns, it gets to observe the psychotic inconsistencies, and
t's gaining a great deal of facility through sheer exercise
rom my calculations. Simply by occupying it we've managed to slow down its destructive action more than the
military did in the whole time it was here."

"Is the answer, then, just finding problems for it to
solve?" Jon asked.

"Again, not so simple. Both Clea and I have been
working on formulating these two problems for years.
Anything you would think of in a week or a month the
machine would probably get through in a few minutes
maximum. We should be finished today, and after that I
don't know what will happen."

Nonik laughed. "I'll just have to go on raving to it."

"That's the one other thing that seems to occupy it,"
Clea said. "Listening to Vol. It's taken to doing a complete sonic and syntactical analysis of everything he says
and running it off against all the experiences it's got
collated."

"But I won't stay put," Vol said. "That's the only
problem, isn't it, Clea?" He moved now to the window
that opened onto one of the roadways. "You see," he
went on, "sometimes I have to go, perhaps just around the
city, but sometimes out of it, back to the City of a
Thousand Suns, or even farther, looking . . . I can't help
it." Suddenly he stepped out on the road and was gone.

"It's terrible what he's going through," Rolth said,
after a moment.

"Clea?" Alter said, "you lost someone you loved
once, just like Vol. You got over it."

"I lost someone once," Clea repeated, "That's how I
know how terrible it is. It took me three years before I was

fit for anything halfway human again. In this way, he's doing much better than I did. He's still making his poems. But he's caught in a confused, chaotic, meaningless, totally," she paused, "random world."

"You said something once," Jon told her, "to a little neanderthal boy, that if you could perceive all the factors, then the random element disappears."

"Don't you think we've tried to tell him that?" Rolth said.

"He tells us to predict the next prime number, and laughs," said Clea.

"And his poems?" Alter asked. "Are they better or worse than before?"

They were silent again. "I can't tell," Rolth said at last. "I suppose I'm just too close to him to be able to judge at all."

"They're much more difficult to understand," Clea said. "And in some ways much simpler. They contain far more objective observation, but the significance of the juxtaposition or imagery, of emotional tone has got so involved that I don't know whether it's magnificently controlled or . . ."

". . . or insane," Rolth finished; she had turned away from the thought.

After practising tumbling for an hour together that evening Jon and Alter wandered up the darkening roadway. They took a stairway that mounted from one road to a higher spiral. As they came out they saw they were above all the buildings save for the central palace. This roadway curved about the dark tower through the night, and from the railing they could look down across the smaller buildings of Telphar.

Below them the city stretched towards the plains and

the plains towards the mountains, which still glowed with the faintly flickering radiation barrier along their snaggled edges. Mercury lights along the roadway flicked on and wiped away their shadows. Looking up, they saw a figure twenty yards ahead, leaning against the railing and looking across the city.

"Were you looking for me?" Nonik asked.

Jon shook his head.

"Sometimes the 'enemy' looks for me," Nonik said. "I go for a walk, thinking I've escaped, when suddenly I hear a voice, out of nowhere, talking to me, telling me it needs me. . . ." The sharp laugh broke from his mouth. "That sounds crazy to you, doesn't it? But I'm talking about something real." He turned away and said loudly, "How are you feeling today, old child of metal insects and silenium crystals!"

A resonant voice came out of the night; "I feel fine, Vol Nonik. But it is night, not day. Is that significant?"

Nonik turned back to them. "Catches you up every time," he said. "Maddening, huh? Whole damned city's rigged. It uses an induction field somewhere about a mile down to shake the metal railing into the vibrations of speech so that this whole guard rail becomes a loudspeaker."

"And it calls you?" Alter asked.

"It?" repeated Nonik. "A thousand, thousand dead men, squeezed in a million transistors, polished and planed to a single voice—calls me. It's hard not to answer. But sometimes"—he looked at his fist about the railing—"I want to get away, where I don't have to speak."

"And someone else," Jon said, "someone else is calling you too?"

Nonik looked up puzzled, and through the mask of puzzlement the laugh broke, but slow and quiet this time. He shook his head. "No, you see I'm a step ahead of Clea and Rolth, just on one point. Prime numbers, or Format's last theorem, or the four-colour map problem, or Gödle's law, it doesn't matter: yes, when we know everything the random disappears, but while we're finding out we still have to deal with it somehow. So the idea of the *random* is a philosophical tool, like *God*, or *The Absurd*, or *Das Umbermench, Existence, Death, Masculine, Feminine,* or *Morality:* they aren't things, they are the names we arbitrarily give to whole areas of things; sharpening-tools for the blade of perception we strike reality with."

"What about your poetry?" Jon asked. "Clea and Rolth say they can't tell whether it's good or bad any more."

"I can," Nonik said. "It's better than I've ever written, than I ever could have written before. And that's the most . . . terrible thing yet I've had to think about." His eyes had dropped, but again they raised to Jon's and Alter's. "Poetry, or anything man makes, even to this city, is set against death. But have you ever watched an animal die slowly? Somewhere, within the process of dying, when it realizes both that its destruction is inevitable and that it is still alive, its cry soars into another, different range, octaves higher, sharp with an unimagined energy. That's where my poems are now. If Rolth and Clea don't understand them it's because they have heard very little music played in this range. . . ." Again he stopped, and the smile returned. ". . . Or it could be because, after all, I am mad. It would be easier to be mad, I think, only to have to call out for help, like my friend here"—he indicated the city—"easier than having to swer. Then, maybe to think madness is easier is itself ad." He shook his head. "You don't know about my ife, do you? I mean, other than that she was killed. You on't know who she was, what sort of a person she was, hat she might have been."

They shook their heads.

"She was an artist," Vol said. "She drew, and she ainted, and we went hunting for clay deposits together on 'arsin Island, and she brought back red clay and made hapes with it that hardened, and grew pale, and were eautiful. For what it meant, there were enough people hat thought her pictures were better than my poems, and ice versa, so that we could both laugh and use the blades of jealousy that shot back and forth to pry open even urther our love. She taught school, I ran a mali gang. We ell in love, and I came to read to her class, and she fled with me through screeching night raids, and we both saw quickly that, under the crumbling lies and hypocrisy, she was forced to be as destructive in her classroom—a prison to exclude ideas that would 'hurt their little minds' and make her lose her job—as I was in the vicious streets; that purely through the upset in the proper places I caused, I was as constructive in my violence as she was allowed to be 'creative' in school. We both had clear visions of ourselves, at least in our art. Our parents refused to admit it existed, and so we had to create our own values for it, by single word and brush-stroke. Our parents saw each of us marrying, settling down, but certainly not with one another. The Toron Museum had bought a portfolio of her drawings—seven had to be excluded for obscenity—and a Royal Fellowship had just come through for my first book—provided I would remove five poems which 'brought undue emphasis to certain regrettable aspects of society, implying governmental laxity'—and we heard of a new City on the mainland; we decided to leave. We had to leave by noon, because a friend who worked as a clerk in the governmental office had held up as long as he could a warrant for my arrest that would have confined me to hard labour in the penal mines for an indefinite period; these 'regrettable aspects of society implying governmental laxity' that I had criticized had caught up on me.

"Only by noon, she was . . ." the words died under the breeze that stroked their hair. "And I was . . . then I *was* insane. But I came back to sanity, carrying voices centuries dumb. I knew the heights I could reach because I had surveyed the nadirs of their foundations. I knew how shallow everything I had written till then was; I knew that till then I had not even written poetry, had not known enough to write poetry. I also saw that her pictures were as shallow as my poems."

Alter frowned. Jon put his arm around her shoulder.

"You see, a poet is wounded into speech, and he examines these wounds, meticulously, to discover how to heal them. The bad poet harangues at the pain and yowls at the weapons that lacerate him; the great poet explores the inflamed lips of ruined flesh with ice-caked fingers, glittering and precise; but ultimately his poem is the echoing, dual voice reporting the damage. Neither of us had been wounded enough, certainly not a wound as deep as the other's destruction. Her sculptures and paintings were as trifling as my former metred utterances. Only if *I* had been the one killed might her work have contained all that mine may contain now." He took a breath, a gulping one. "That's why I hope I'm mad. That's why I hope what I'm doing now is drivel from the lunatic brain. I say I think my poems now are finer than anything I've ever done; I only ope that is the judgement of a ruined mind, with critical aculties shocked and fragmented on grief; because if they re great"—he whispered here, and looked away over the buildings—"they cost too much! To feed on destruction, bloating to greatness . . . they're not worth it!" The last words hissed.

Something snapped in Jon. He felt it go, and saw that Alter felt it as his fingers tightened on her arm. He dropped his hand, bewildered at the thing surging in his mind, like a memory coming to the surface of turbid froth. He stepped backwards, not sure whether to fight it down, not sure how to accept it. He started to run back down the roadway. Something had already begun to form in the cool vaults of his brain, flashing like a power-blade thrust up from the dark.

Alter cried after him, then turned to Vol. "Nonik, please . . ." They followed.

When he burst into the control room Clea and Rolth looked up in surprise. "I . . ." Jon started.

Alter and Nonik reached the room seconds later. "Are you all right, Jon?" Alter cried, but he whirled and caught her by the shoulders, and turned her slowly around him. Nonik, bewildered, stepped back with Clea and Rolth.

"I want you to tell"—each word came with its own breath, as the thought wrestled with articulation—"tell me something. You see, there was a plan, to stop a war. Only . . . only the people who made both the war and the plan are dead now! Alter, you and I, we were part of the plan. And when they died, you and I, we tried to stop, but we couldn't, we had to go on with it, all the way here to Telphar, even though they were dead . . . like we were slaves!"—he took another breath—"like *prisoners*! We were part of the plan to stop the war, but you, Clea and Rolth, you were part of the war: no, I know you were tricked into it, but you were still part of it. Clea, you *did* help build the computer, and Rolth, you *knew* what state the empire was in. You could have spoken out about it, given the same sort of help you gave to the City of a Thousand Suns when you passed through. No, don't say anything. It doesn't matter now.'' He released Alter's shoulders. ''I don't know what you were, Vol; the gratuitous, still point in the random world, or the random observer in a world whose order is self-destructive; that doesn't matter either. But me? To me, that matters, who I am; a clumsy kid, a prisoner, who is free now, and a man, and not so clumsy. Well, I have to ask you''—he turned to Alter, and touched her shoulders again—''you, because you've taught me, and I love you''—he turned to Clea, Catham, and Nonik—''you because you've taught me, and I respect you. . . .'' Suddenly he whirled and screamed at the wall of dials, ''. . . And you too, if you can answer me, because you've taught me too, and I hate you!'' He paused, shaking and angry, waiting for the machine to destroy him, as it had destroyed the ''aggressive'' wrench Catham had hurled at it: three blue lights merely turned red. Jon looked back again. ''In this random, chaotic world, filled with apes and demigods and all in between, where mass-murder and assassination is the pastime of the hour, where any structure you cling to may topple in a moment, where a City of a Thousand Suns may be destroyed by a machine commanded by the psychosis of an empire and beauty doubts itself as insanity gorged on death—and I am free''—again he drew in his breath—''*what* am I free to do? *You tell me what I am free to do!*''

And a universe away a city on a desert under a double sun was in confusion:

"The agents from Earth, will they arrive? . . ."

"But one of them's dead. The Duchess has already been killed. . . ."

"The other three, two of them are together at one end of the transit-ribbon, the other is hiding in rubble of the palace at the other end. . . ."

"This war, will we win it, or lose it . . ."

"The *Lord of the Flames*, where is he? You said that of the four of them he would constantly be in one. . . ."

"The *Lord of the Flames*, you said he would betray them to one another. How has he hurt them, which one is he in . . . ?"

"The *Lord of the Flames*, will he come to us, will we be able to fight him, will we be able to win . . . ?"

The Triple-Being made a calming gesture. They quieted. *We still have time before the agents from Earth arrive. True, one has been killed, and the telepath, Arkor, is still in Toron. . . .*

"You said," interrupted one voice, "that the *Lord of the Flames* would be moving from one to another of them, sabotaging each one in turn. Which one is it in now, how has it done this?"

"Is it in Jon?" asked another. "Is this why he asks this preposterous question?"

The Triple-Being laughed. *It attacked Jon first, then it was in Alter; it inhabited the Duchess just before her death; now it is crouching with Arkor in the ruins of the palace.*

"But why?"

"What did it make them do?"

"How did they betray?"

As the Lord of the Flames *has been observing this war,* answered the Triple-Being, *so we have been observing him, and we have discovered a great deal about him. You remember we said that he was a completely alien form of life, such that ideas like murder, compassion, intelligence were foreign to him. Well, now we are close enough to understand why this is and what exactly the basic difference between him and all of us here is. The essential factor in all our make-ups is that we are individuals, and as individuals, we are alone. Even those of us with telepathy are alone, for they are still working only with images. Even beings so closely linked as the three lobes of our intelligence, are basically individual and alone. It is both our salvation and our damnation, and opposed to it is the desire inherent in our aloneness to move closer to another individual, or individuals, to perceive with them, through them, to unite somehow. Many of you dual or multisexual species have this internalized into your procreative rituals. Even the monosexual creatures preserve it in syzygy. The ultimate in aloneness in each of your cultures is death. Many of you have symbiotic relationships where when one individual is completely separated from all others he will physically die.*

In the Lord of the Flames, *however, this polarity between the isolation of the individual and his desire to be united with other individuals is reversed. It goes back to the very nature of his physical make-up, and its ramifications are as subtle as they are throughout the species of this universe. First of all, he is composed of the energies created by plasmas of matter and anti-matter held in stasis. He is a collective consciousness in which the individuals are not alone, even physically, for their energies are constantly shifting and interchanging. Anti-matter*

151

and matter, as those of you whose cultures have reached atomic physics know, annihilate one another if brought into contact. As we equate aloneness and isolation with death, so it equates bringing individuals—individuals who are already in energetic unison—together as death, for when this happens their actual physical beings explode. Conversely, reproduction takes place not by bringing individuals together but by separating them, so that they re-create themselves on the basis through which matter and anti-matter are propagated when energy travels through a gravitational field. The ramifications of this reverse polarity in its attitudes towards life and behaviour are infinite.

"And this being is preparing to make war on us?" asked one delegate to the City.

Apparently. But we are still a good deal ahead of it. It has not discovered that our life process has nothing to do with the stasis of matter and anti-matter; anti-matter is so rare in this universe that the chances of life hinging on it are impossibly low. One of the reasons the Lord of the Flames is concentrating on Toromon so heavily is that the basic source of power is tetron, a radioactive crystal of uranium in conjunction with radioactive iodine. The fusion can only occur under atomic temperatures, as a great deal of Toromon was exposed to back in what they call the Great Fire. The balance of the two elements creates a much more controllably radioactive material, and the amount of fugitive anti-matter in the process is tremendous compared to the occasional positron or anti-proton that result from cosmic-ray bombardment. The Lord of the Flames is sure he will find the secret of our life form in the civilization using the greatest amount of anti-matter. That's the chemistry of it. On the higher level he is also *trying to discover how our behaviour under attack differs from his: in other words, what is a war to us.*

"Does this polarity you tell us about affect the way we fight?"

It certainly does.

"More important, how does this polarity affect the way the *Lord of the Flames* will behave in battle?"

Ultimately, the social traumas that cause war are those which promote the greatest isolation of the greatest number of individuals that still keep them in physical proximity. Disaster, famine, insupportable distribution of goods, exploitation, increased population till enough individuals are denied the opportunity of being together, fulfilling their yearning towards oneness with all other individuals. In most of your cultures, even the most egalitarian, the sexes are separated during battle.

"Compensated for by a huge rise in copulation/population right afterwards," commented one delegate.

Precautionary, stated the Triple-Being. *But the whole strategy of war as we know it takes advantage of the aloneness of man: hit your enemy in his most dispersed forces; isolate a troop and you can destroy it. Well, all of these factors are entirely reversed in fighting the Lord of the Flames. If you can drive as many of its elements as possible together they will annihilate themselves, whereas actual isolation makes them physically reproduce; to separate one individual component of the Lord of the Flames from the rest would mean you were pitted against a force that was multiplying as you attacked, would overwhelm you before you could harm it. Just as we are alone, yearning to come together, so all its components are part of one another, yearning to be alone. Just as the traumas*

*that cause us to fight are the traumas that cause us to be
alone, so its idea of a destructive act is one——*

"—that brings individuals together!" One of the delegates was ecstatic "I see it now, now I see what it's been
doing on Earth, with Toromon!"

Please allow me to continue——

"But I understand now——"

*Please. The first attempt of the Lord of the Flames to
press individuals together was when it increased the radiation barrier, driving the original inhabitants of Telphar
back to the coast and to Toron. But the elements of war
were already fermenting in the culture. Its second attempt
was when the war broke out; instead of letting Toromon
discover an external enemy to fight it fostered the idea of
the computer, that would physically hold the inhabitants
together while they were under the illusion that they were
fighting far-flung battles. When our agents on Earth managed to expose this to the people the result was that
moment of telepathic contact that blanketed the empire.
During this moment every individual in Toromon learned
something, and so did the Lord of the Flames. What they
learned was exactly how alone they were. A few minds
were able to deal with it, profit from it, learn from it how
they might come together. But for most the result was
terror, and chaos. And the Lord of the Flames began to
get some inkling of how humanity, and ultimately how life
in our universe, works. By this time, to give our agents all
over a fair chance to learn also, we had several times put
you all in as close empathetic contact as we could simu-
late. Then we brought each one of you individually to the
City and even gave you a five dimensional view of what-
you-would-have-been-if. We hoped that this contact might
help you all in rallying your forces when and if the final
conflict came.*

But now the Lord of the Flames *is examining Earth, and particularly Toromon, under a microscope. It has centered its observations directly on our four agents, and instead of acts that would shove the entire society in on itself, it concentrated on urging individuals together, and observed the results. First it attacked Jon, urged him to go back to his father.*

"Then it made Alter meet her aunt?" suggested one of the delegates who had been meticulously following the discussion.

No, answered the Triple-Being. *In a world where individuals are alone no two approach the same experience from the same direction. Alter's reconciliation with her aunt was not at all the same thing to her that Jon's was to his father. The* Lord of the Flames *forced her to speak with the mad queen, who was about to kill them: that's what it did to her. Then it went on to the Duchess of Petra. It made her not only go with the young King but for a moment accept his ideas, which were so at odds with her own: even though they died moments later, perhaps it learned the most from her. Now it has moved into Arkor's mind, though he doesn't know it, and waits with him in the palace ruins. He has still to be urged to his encounter.*

"What has the *Lord of the Flames* learned from each of them?"

So far it has learned that coming together makes them more able to bear the aloneness, more able to come together with others. It still, however, does not fully understand why this aloneness is objectionable in the first place when for it, it is the one thing desired.

"But the poems . . . ?"

"The unified field-theory . . . ?"

"The history . . . ?"

"You said if they can get these to us before the *Lord of*

the Flames gets them, then we will know the outcome of this greater war?''

Well, answered the Triple-Being, *Jon and Alter are only minutes away from the possession of all three, and the* Lord of the Flames *is at the other end of the empire from them.*

"They still must get here," reminded one cynical delegate, "and an empire is not a very long distance to a creature that can step galaxies in microseconds."

That is very true, said the Triple-Being, echoing itself in its triad voice. The sand shifted across the desert as night came slowly over the white world and the double shadows lengthened. *Let us watch.*

A universe away, Rolth Catham frowned and said, "Well, Jon, I suppose"—he paused—"I suppose each person has to answer that question for himself."

"No!" This was from Alter. "You have to tell him . . . us . . . me, something. You have to! Otherwise, what are you good for? Don't you see, you have to be able to tell us something!"

Rolth shook his head. "I can't."

"Well, try," this from Vol, followed by tense, quiet laughter that hung his words ambiguously between urgent imperative and insane command.

"Clea?" Alter said. "Don't you remember, you told me once, back when we both worked at the circus together, you once told me that to be able to justify yourself to others was the most important thing in the world when you were too sick to justify yourself to yourself. Well, I don't know, but if that's true, but . . . well, can't you say something now?"

Clea looked confused, her dark brows contracting. "All I can think of is . . . you're free to be anything you want, a mathematician, a historian, a poet"—Vol laughed again—"anything we're free to be."

Jon shook his head. "That's not good enough. I'm not a stupid man, I've got a certain amount of physical strength, I've got a certain amount of mental and physical discipline, but I'm not an artist or an economist, or a scientist, and to talk about my being free to be one is like talking about my hitching up a moth-drawn chariot and flying into the sun."

Something behind the wall of dials began to click and several lights changed colour.

"Well, you transistorized baby with electronic tapeworm, you have an answer for him?" Vol asked.

The reply was laconic: "No." But the clicking continued. A panel opened in the wall, and three piles of paper were revealed.

"Rolth," said Clea in surprise, "it must be finished with the collation processing."

Rolth picked up one of the piles of paper: "*Looms of the Sea,*" he read, "*The Final Revision of the History of Toromon,* I think that's an awfully good title. I just hope the theory holds up." He picked up the second sheaf. "Here's your unified field theory, Clea."

She took the pages. "What's the third pile?" she asked.

"I asked the computer would it make up a copy of all of Vol's poems it had access too. I wanted a copy." He picked up the sheaf of poems. His naked brain gleamed grey behind the plastic. He frowned and turned back to Jon. "If you were an artist, or a scientist, then maybe I could help you decide what you were free to do."

"That's a start," Vol said. "I'm listening."

"Basically, it would just be free to commit yourself to your work, or not to; and then, to commit your work to man, or not to . . . no, not to man, but to a concept of what man might be."

"All right," Vol said, "you're talking to me and Clea now. You've got to explain that."

"I mean this. When you write a poem, Vol, you write it to an ideal reader, one who will hear all the rhythmical subtleties, will respond to all the images, will reverberate to all the references, will even be able to catch you when you do something wrong; this reader is the one you labour for when you spend hours to make sure each line is perfect. Now you can be sure that in this world there are not very many of those around, but you have to believe that he could exist: even more, that any man of the street with the proper training could be educated to be that ideal reader. If you didn't believe in him you wouldn't try to write perfect poems. When Clea propounds a theory she tries to make it as clear and as rigorous as she can. She knows that a good many people won't be able to read through it and make anything at all out of it, but she checks and rechecks it for the one person who will be able to contain the whole concept of it. The same way I check and recheck my historical theory for cultural, sexual, emotional bias, for that ideal man, who is ideally unbiased. To commit yourself to this concept doesn't mean that with your work you try to teach people how to be ideal. That's propaganda, and since most of the artists and scientists are pretty far from ideal themselves, they are more or less defeated at the start if they take that tack. It's rather to acknowledge that man, with all this chaos, even so, can be ideal, and to make your work worthy of him."

Now Vol turned to Jon. "Where does that leave you?"

"Free to try and achieve that ideal, or not to try," Jon said. "But we get our blueprints more or less from you three."

Vol laughed once more.

"Will the machine make copies of those things for you?"

"Of course," Clea said. "Why?"

"I'd like copies of all of them," Jon said, "just to see how close I come to the ideal reader."

Puzzled, Clea pressed a button on the console, and the cabinet began to fill again with pages. "Is the transit-ribbon from this end open, Clea?" he asked.

"It was closed at the palace," Alter reminded him.

"Can it be opened from this end?"

"As a matter of fact it can," Clea said.

"I want to do some reading, and maybe get on the way to becoming that ideal reader of yours." He turned to Alter. "And I want to find Arkor."

"The telepath?" Catham asked.

"That's right," Jon said.

"What for?"

"Something about perception," Jon said. He hefted the papers in his hand. "I want to take these to him—give him a chance to try his hand at the ideal readership—and see if maybe he can't figure out a . . . problem."

"Problem?" asked Catham.

Jon nodded. "What the next problem after these will have to be. And when I—we—get it we'll be back with it, for the computer."

While Clea was checking out the transit-ribbon, Jon and Alter told Nonik of their journey. Now he leaned on the railing and shook his head. "But is any of it real?" he said. "Don't you stop to wonder that?"

Jon and Alter looked puzzled.

"We all exist only in the mind of God, so some ancient thought. We are the psychotic quips of a deranged cosmic mind, perhaps? Maybe a highly neurotic mind, a bit suicidal, tending towards a manic-depressive cycle; isn't that the one which defines my existence?'' he laughed. ''Shafts of divine insight!'' Now he spat over the railing. ''Or maybe just in each other's minds, that's where we exist. Are you really anything at all worth considering. Jon Koshar? Or are you only the story a bunch of prisoners recall of a boy they never knew. Does your white hair, your dark skin, your dawn-grey eyes encompass the real you, Alter Koshar? Or are you the projection of children gasping before a circus poster where someone has sketched you sequined and distorted in midflight on a trampoline?''

''I think it's about time to go back,'' Jon said, a little uncomfortably.

''Time to go,'' Nonik echoed. ''Oh, yes, time to go.''

In the laboratory, Clea said: ''It's still functioning; somehow, with all those bombs the ribbon is still connected. I don't know what you'll find at the other end, but get on the stage.'' They climbed up the metal stairway and stood below the crystal. Jon had the papers under his arm, and Alter's hand rested in his.

Clea stepped to a tetron-unit, pushed a switch; somewhere a solenoid hummed, and the first row of scarlet-knobbed switches in a bank of forty-nine swung from ''off'' to ''on.''

''I want to go too!'' Vol Nonik suddenly said.

''You can't go now,'' Clea said. ''It isn't set up to carry that much.''

The next row of switches swung to ''on.''

''I've got to get out of this stainless-steel asylum!'' Nonik said, shaking his head. Then his eyes caught fixedly on the forms that had begun to shimmer on the stage.

"We'll send you as soon as we finish sending them, if you want." Catham said. "With over a certain weight you can't predict the molecular destination taken through the——"

Without warning, Nonik let out a howl and leapt forward. He vaulted with his one good hand to the lip of the stage and staggered beneath the crystal.

"Vol . . . !"

And then something flared white beneath the bulb. A small buss snapped with a loud pop and a fall of sparks.

"What happened!" demanded Rolth.

"The stupid . . ." Clea began. "Now I don't know what happened. It's just set built to carry that much weight at once. I don't know whether they'll get there, or even where they'll end up. Or if they'll even all get there at once!"

The platform was empty.

CHAPTER TWELVE

ARKOR lay on a pile of cloth in the corner of the laboratory-tower, looking at the sunlight falling through the broken ceiling.

The huge crystal at the end of the transit-ribbon began to glow: then Vol Nonik stumbled to the rail—screaming.

The bruised body Arkor took in at a glance. The pattern of the mind leaped through the room and quivered hungrily before him; Arkor pulled back. Hurt, injury, the long cords of pain shaking and disonant. A circuit of careful parts and patterning, precise and tremendous, yet here and there welded open or shorted out from its own heat; a painting so vivid in detail and colour that its own intensity had charred the canvas. Arkor tried to turn away mentally. "What do you want?" he asked, sitting up.

The figure shook his head. "I don't want to talk any more, I just don't want to . . . speak."

"You don't have to talk," Arkor said. "What do you want?" Nonik stared with gleaming eyes. "All right," Arkor said. "Come on, then." Vol followed him across the floor and to the door of the chamber: he couldn't shut all of the mind's crying out. Practised in rhythms, it turned wailing against itself as they climbed down the stairs to the yard.

. . . the motion of my body through smoke trickling from the broken wall recalls a clumsy behemoth in cool tides; the sun falls through the ceiling in a wide band across the steps, and at my glance the wounded giant broke off from my gaze, the shimmering points jutting in the haze, violence of sill and portal as we pass the wrecked street's agony, corded lips still before smashed masonry, the stumps of ruined dreams; O, these caverns that I cannot crawl, anguished at evening, empty of ruined dreams, machines sprung under evening's hammers, backward-bounding mind mounting to tongue fire against a ribbon on the sky. . . .

Arkor watched Vol stumble ahead of him along the blasted pavement of the Avenue of the Oysture, thinking, what's one good reason why I should bother to follow either his broken mind or his broken body? But he followed, and two blocks later Nonik turned, his eyes risen to the charred sky-line, and Arkor tried to block out what pounded at him from Nonik's mind.

162

. . . the fall of the towers, O ancient Christ, the fall of the towers, and the bared knife belly-buried and streaming, the fall of the towers, I can hear her screaming, I can see her hands twisting to get free, her body arched backward, skin split, bladder loose with blood, dust and crumbled masonry, a flood of refuse in the street, screaming, her small hands coming out to meet my larger hand, brick and iron twisting to get free, the fall of the towers, my standard and support shattered, my heart jarred loose, her violence looped in a thick noose of struts, electric cable, mortar, brick. . . .

"What do you want?" Arkor whispered again, and Nonik, his cheeks wet, looked back. "Tell me," Arkor said. "It would be easier for me to give it to you than to listen to this." Fear burned in Nonik's eyes; he turned and fled. It was easy to follow him, however. The thoughts chattered like static through the ruined streets.

. . . a flaming woman sits in the throne of my eyes; a bronze gigantic bird thrown wingward on the ruptured field crashed the iron fence that shields the chewed-up asphalt of the aircraft field; the hard knot of desire loosens, sprawls open by the long, bleak hive-house walls, male and female, embattled and become epicene, magnificent, and one: rage, and now three, five, seven, terror rips apart the wild iambic madness of the fleeing child, chaotic shards form patterings, eleven, thirteen, infinite and prime, ordered, unpredictable as rhyme: a young boy flings a rock down from the roof, vicious it cuts my thigh; what greater proof of innocence or compassion, as suddenly my eye holds for a shocked breath his startled eye; night walkers stalk the wharfs at sunset, scavengers hiding in the shadow of the slant launch siding, they see me, run over the cobbles, pause, gaze, turn, hurry off, I am alone, walking the piers, as my eyes chase the grey deflated hunger to consume the sea-waves' sepulchred wind-weaving loom. . . .

"Wake up," Arkor said. Nonik uncurled beside the wall like a sick cat. Arkor wanted to say *wake up and shut up.* How do you tell someone to stop thinking. "I've got a boat for you, like you wanted." He waited for the emotions which roared at him to resolve themselves in Nonik's face. They walked to the pier where Arkor had found the boat, deserted and fuelled. From the wheelhouse he watched Nonik look up at the transit-ribbon under the new moon.

. . . a whip of metal, beautiful and free, from crumpled struts leaps the crushed-foil sea, while here we stare the dark troughs lashing back along the ocean's churning nightward track, violated in depth, runnelled by keel, droplets suspended on a wire wheel, time crushed by the pressure of light and muscle, ground to discrete fragments between the sky and sand, while distant bulkhead shadows block the stars: fools and their floating gardens in the moon, raised high on aluminium pontoons, precipitate above a wave, trapped below genesis, spilled in the fall to silt fonds, a jewel-heavy skull through whose wet sockets the tetras flush, whose bone-holes acknowledge completion and redemption, polar action and evil, meridial death and love. . . .

"Where do you think you're going to go like this, Vol?"

"I . . . I don't. . . ."

. . . picture my hand palm-stripped, the red harp of sinew caught on no music vulnerable, vaulted in no engine. . . .

"Where are you running, Vol Nonik? Don't say you don't know, I won't take it."

"I . . . I . . ."

. . . don't want to talk, and the picture of my face—red chalk on brown paper—burned and charred till the beautiful is released and the responsible furies rage. . . .

When they docked on the mainland, after a few minutes, Nonik left the rail, glanced once at the transit-ribbon, then walked up the beach. The wind scoured sand from dune tops and threw it over the weathered walls of a deserted fisherman's cottage. The door lay on the ground, and through the window an abandoned loom set half strung. They walked farther through the empty village. *You are trapped in that bright moment where you learned your doom* was scribbled across the sagging wall of an ice-house.

. . . echo and re-echo, caught, held, and released, the cry of wild pigeons, and some stranger beast, crystalline and timorous, treads leaves and dried vines to the metal bottom of my mind, and the first words come back, a cupric gleam, the walls of perception shaken, this vile voice not art, but madness trapped by ritual patternings of sound, lying because the ritual is bound by the limp nerves' response, the total matrix trying to contain realities of heart and gut and brain, knowing this working realness is only a machine constructed to apprehend the real; and the existence of leaf, sand, light, and good flicker out as they are named by the beast before me, followed and fleeing, stumbling by trees, beach, beneath sun and morning, flung with the mind against the veined rock, the mirror breaks, again the beast awakes, stepping lazily from the splinters, stretching claws, preening glass-black

eathers, whispering of weights world-age old, lisping
leath-deeds that cringle, gnash, shock new speech from
he struck tongue; I will walk down the muscular anger of
my voice, I will trample silence under the leaves; my
lands before me fill with rushing sun spots shaken through
he forest as I run: I will find new barriers, I will brush
hem back with burning hands. . . .

"Eat," Arkor said.

Nonik leaned his head on the tree, shook it twice, and
turned away.

Arkor waited a moment. When he was certain, flung the
food back into the fire. "Look, the City of a Thousand
Suns is that way. Over there are the penal mines." He
paused long enough to see Nonik look up to where the
transit-ribbon gleamed above the trees. "You want to go
back to Telphar?"

But Nonik shook his head and lurched forward.

. . . these turreted cities at noon are the mind's ruined
images, perfection, death, and transition—skewered on
fishbones to the streets' stone siding, where gated trees
shake thunderous fleaces at the sky and children cry and
change—we are leaving the long chancels of the forest for
the broken rocks, the ossific trunks, rutts in the shaling
ground, we are driving for a landscape more profound, yet
in the lavid runnels memories of green are precious as her
mouth brushing the back of my neck, these plains scattered with yesterday's death, where I seek yesterday's
dying, crushed trunks of petrified trees; I can see heat
lightning, over the dead city sinestral as charred bone,
circling the stone like a myth, and as I round the webbed
towers of the cancerous dream, left-bent and gravid with

her death, I am leaving also the illusion that I am alone, the giant, the beast in the mirror, the metallic wind clanging the rocks, or silent as slain rats bowled belly-upward on the ground; I will not look at the concupiscent city, I will not walk in the violent streets, nor even in the ruins where the dextral ghosts of this race gamble near leather windows and crouch before flightless stairs or watch a stubborn orchard of gnarled kharba; these, land-locked, atavistic, have none of the sea's austerity, only the wrecked sands of an idea without voice, a world without vision; know then this journey seeks to define ends, seeks shores where farther oceans start; caged by the over-muscled heart, we are trapped in that bright moment where we learned our doom, but still we struggle, knowing, too, that freedom is imposed the very moment when the trap springs. . . .

"Stop it," Arkor said.

Evening burnished the crusted plain. Telphar was behind them.

"Stop it," Arkor said. "You're going to die."

Nonik shook his head hard once; then he began to laugh, till the laugh faded into a whisper: ". . . die?" He shook his head again. ". . . the trap springs closed. The barrier . . ."

"We've already passed the edge of the barrier," Arkor said.

Bronze light gouged and pried among the naked stones around them.

"You'll die too!"

Arkor shook his head. "I can take much more radiation than you can."

For the first time a definite emotion seated itself in

Nonik's features. He frowned: "Have I gone too far already?"

"Turn around and come back to me, Vol?"

Nonik began to laugh again. "But you can't even see it. I mean the limit, the place past which I can't come back. Is it here? Am I standing on it?"

Suddenly he sprinted ahead thirty feet. "Don't you see," he called back, "perhaps I've just passed it." He began to walk slowly back to Arkor over the empty, desolate rock. "That means I'm dead already. Every cell in my body is already dead, but maybe for an hour I'll be able to stagger around, pretending to be alive. I'm dead. This is how it feels to be dead. I'll go blind first, and then I'll stagger as though I'm very drunk." He brushed his good hand over his face. "Is it starting? I . . . I thought it was going dim." Suddenly he grabbed Arkor's shoulder and cried out, "No!"

Arkor seized the small, shaking human in his great hands. The quivering, glittering mind turned under his own mind. "Vol, come back," he said. "I see so much more than you. You know so much, and so little. You can't be free if . . . if you're dead."

Nonik pulled back abruptly; fear filled his face, the face of a girl filled his mind. He turned, scrambled up the slope, and ran forward again. Slowly the chaos quieted as Vol ran farther into the rocks.

Arkor turned in the ocean of stone and began to walk back. Alone again, the telepathic giant cried.

EPILOGUE

EPILOGUE

BEETLES . . . carbuncle . . . silver . . . Jon sucked the sharpness of ozone. Alter caught his hand as she gazed down the white sand. With the sudden change in gravity, Jon nearly dropped the papers, but Alter helped him catch them up. They looked again towards the city where:

Smoke fell like silver scales through the shell of the royal palace of Toron. The stumps of the city's towers jammed at the sky. People still huddled in the streets, but many had already started to make their way to the shore. Some helped one another over the girders and fallen masonry that choked the street. Some moved by themselves. But they were moving.

Alter pressed back against him; but Jon put his free hand around her shoulder and started down the dunes. Light struck through their bodies. They moved like ambient glass.

"Have they brought the history——"

"—the unified field theory——"

"—the poems?" the delegates in the city demanded with a flood of questioning:

"Have they come?"

"Will we win the war?"

"Where is the *Lord of the Flames*?"

And the triple answer: *There is no war!*

Jon and Alter, hand in hand, paused, listening, at the edge of the City.

The Lord of the Flames, continued the Triple-Being, *has observed enough to know that war would be useless, and that if it came to war both sides would be wiped out.*

171

"We would destroy each other?" Jon asked.

We would each destroy ourselves first, corrected the Triple-Being.

"Destroy ourselves?" Alter asked, "But how?" Wonder grew in them like deserts flowering suddenly beneath longed-for and familiar rain.

Beyond a certain amount of injury, life cannot exist. To desire as much destruction as a war would be such an injury. And if the injury is too great self-destruction may be necessary. Suicide is the safety valve for the sickness to dispose of itself.

Questioning, Jon and Alter approached the city, and before them they saw—

a rocky plain where Vol Nonik staggered, went on his knees, then fell forward and lay still, eyes sunken and black, neck puffy, face distended. Behind him was the silhouette of Telphar on the horizon, and as they watched, it suddenly flared, flamed, and billows of smoke rose from its falling towers

And the Triple-Being said, *That was Earth. The same thing has happened all over the universe.*

"But what?" asked Jon.

The same thing that drove Nonik to suicide, caused the computer to bomb itself out of existence. The wound has at least been cauterized, and you may go home now, and attempt to heal.

"And the *Lord of the Flames*?"

The last random factor has been observed and put in place. And there was triple laughter. *You might say it realizes now that as different as it is from us, it is still akin to us, in that it, too, has this death outlet, and recognizes its kinship. Now it will go on searching, and there will be no war.*

"Then we can go back?" from all the delegates to the city.

And Jon whispered, "To reach the stars," and her hair brushed his face as she bent smiling to him.

before them was the City of a Thousand Suns, beautiful on the lake's edge, and as they watch, Lug's neanderthal family might arrive, and Catham and Clea trudge tiredly along the edge of the lake to the City, and from the other side an elderly couple, tattered and exhausted, might also gain the City: perhaps Rara, and Old Koshar; and the tall figure of Arkor might move towards the low buildings from one side, while the figure of a forest woman, also with the triple scars of the telepath, may approach from the other, their minds having already joined and touched, experience and perception weighed against experience and perception, the music their minds made free in the double sound of their names, Arkor, Larta, that they sang to one another, all, some, or none, the choice random, and left not to chance but to you

Free to build or destroy they, too, approached the City of a Thousand Suns, to be struck by blue smoke, dispersed by sudden lightning, dropped from a web of silver fire . . . the red of polished carbuncle . . . the green of beetles' wings . . .

New York
February 28th, 1964

AUTHOR'S AFTERWORD

"ANYONE," SAID Oscar Wilde, "can write a three-volume novel. All it takes is a complete ignorance of Art and Life." Some seventy years later I was walking across the Brooklyn Bridge with a brilliant poet with waist-length honey hair and eyes that look brown at first but hold copper, green, and yellow. We held hands, watching the cables wheel over us—some months previously we had been married, helping to bring the average nuptial age of the country to its ludicrous all-time low of nineteen —discussing in mute voices that dilemma all such young marrieds must grapple: "All right, what would *you* put into a novel, I mean a real honest to goodness novel?"

The answers came thick and popping: social scope, characterizations, scenes, ideas, experiences we had not read yet but would like to have read. By the time we'd reached the other side of the bridge, we had also reached the flat conclusion that it couldn't possibly all go into one book. It might conceiveably be crowded into three. "You remember what Oscar Wilde said," she reminded me.

Of course I didn't, but I wouldn't let on. That evening I wrote the first chapter of *Out of the Dead City* (Later to be called *Captives of the Flame*.) and planned the last chapter of *City of a Thousand Suns*. Over the next two years I orchestrated, harmonized, conducted, rapped knuckles, coaxed, yelled, threatened suicide, praised extravagantly, criticized coolly, gave amateur psychotherapy: finally the ideas, incidents, and characters of that first chapter had staggered all the way through to the last.

The poet brushes the back of my neck with a touch like a dove stumbling into you, breast first. She looks over my shoulder, and I remember the quiet, cuttingly accurate comments like, "That's wrong," and sometimes, "That's right," and occasionally, "I don't agree but there's room for argument." Then we sit and wonder about all the things that still couldn't go in. There was the scene where the telepath Larta helps a group of mainland farmers outwit a buyer from the city; then, when the farmers discover her telepathy, they stone her. It got lost between Volumes Two and Three.

There was an argument, never written down, between Nonik and the soldier Curly that took place when Nonik was rejected from the army and Curly was accepted: "Even if a man can't control anything else," the poet insisted, "he should at least be able to control when he dies. That's all he's free to do." When he repeated this to Catham, the historian smiled and said, "Ancient religious sceptics spent a great deal of time demanding miracles to establish the existence of a God, that rocks should fly upward and fire burn without fuel. They never realized that what was miraculous was simply that no matter how chaotic and random everything seemed, rocks fell and fires went out at predictable speeds within predictable times." "I don't see the connection," was Nonik's reply. "Think about it till you do," said Catham. For what it's worth, Vol never did see, and at the end, though he is in control—so to speak—of his death, Catham is in control of his life. So there.

Clea and Alter, when they met in Telphar, spent a great deal of time, and had much fun, making plans for a circus in the *City of a Thousand Suns*, which, if chance and the reader allow, they will eventually do.

But these scenes fell before the laws of orchestration.

"The title and the epigraph," the poet reminds me.

Oh, yes, the title of all three books together, "The Fall of the Towers," was lifted from a group of drawings a friend of mine once did depicting different groups of people reacting to some catastrophic incident never shown. The drawings were unfortunately destroyed. I hope he does not begrudge my salvaging the name.

The epigraph for all three books is from the first of W. H. Auden's series of poems on the right of the group to kill.

New York
March 24th, 1964

WINNER OF
THE HUGO AWARD
AND THE
NEBULA AWARD
FOR BEST
SCIENCE FICTION
NOVEL OF
THE YEAR

FRITZ LEIBER

SCIENCE FICTION from the GREAT YEARS

*0157Q	**Alien Planet** Pratt 75¢
*02938	**Armageddon 2419 A.D.** Nowlan $1.25
06713	**The Blind Spot** Hall & Flint $1.50
07690	**The Brain-Stealers** Leinster $1.50
07840	**A Brand New World** Cummings $1.25
27291	**The Galaxy Primes** Smith $1.25
52831	**Metropolis** Von Harbou $1.25
53870	**The Moon Is Hell** Campbell 95¢
70301	**The Radio Beasts** Farley $1.50
70320	**The Radio Planet** Farley $1.50
75431	**Science Fiction—The Great Years Part II** Pohl $1.50
75894	**Sentinels from Space** Russell $1.50
*84331	**The Ultimate Weapon** Campbell $1.25
87182	**War Against the Rull** Van Vogt $1.50

Available wherever paperbacks are sold or use this coupon.

SAMUEL R. DELANY

*04594	Babel 17 $1.50
19683	Einstein Intersection $1.50
20571	The Ballad of Beta2/Empire Star $1.25
22642	The Fall of the Towers $1.95
39021	Jewels of Aptor 75¢

ROGER ZELAZNY

37468	Isle of the Dead $1.50
16704	The Dream Master $1.50
24903	Four For Tomorrow $1.50
80694	This Immortal $1.50

PHILIP JOSÉ FARMER

05360	Behind the Walls of Terra $1.25
78652	The Stone God Awakens $1.25
89238	The Wind Whales of Ishmael $1.25

Available wherever paperbacks are sold or use this coupon.